LOVE YOU SO MADLY

LOVE YOU SO, BOOK 2

TARA LAIN

TARA LAIN BOOKS

LOVE YOU SO MADLY

What does it mean when you have it all ... and you'd like to give some of it back?

Ben Shane's a hard-working guy, deeply committed to an important job.

Dusty Kincaid is a hard-working guy who happens to be Ben's handyman.

Ben's chafing against his engagement to a super-wealthy man who makes him feel like a trophy wife – but is he really going to give up a partner who drives a Ferrari for one who takes the bus?

Dusty has challenges Ben can't begin to imagine, and the world thinks they're crazy. But face it. From the beginning, this love has been a little bit mad.

LOVE YOU SO MADLY is an improbable love, challenged hero, no-sugar-diet, MM romance.

To all the people who live their lives with the mysteries of epilepsy—here's to many happy ever afters.

CHAPTER ONE

OH MY freaking god. I'm mad.

Ben Shane forced his eyes back to his computer screen so he wouldn't stare at him. *Him.*

Outside the huge glass wall of his office, across the aisle in his admin's cubicle, the handyman crawled on his knees under the desk, ratting out some kind of wire and cord nightmare. His blue T-shirt had pulled from his jeans and showed off two exquisite inches of creamy beige, slightly muscled, zero-fatted skin.

Ben swallowed hard and released his breath long and slow, contracting his lungs as he couldn't quite contract lower parts of his anatomy. *Perfection.* Wide shoulders narrowing down the middle of his back like a roadway to even finer things—tiny waist, round butt. And yet he wasn't big. Dusty Kincaid—Ben had casually asked his admin the guy's name—couldn't stand more than five eight with those lean muscles, like maybe a swimmer or long-distance runner. He bounced around ClearWater Technologies shedding sunshine into every corner, seemingly undaunted by all levels of stress and hysteria over impending deadlines and missed product releases. Apparently his job was simple. He was a gofer, handyman, box filler, and carrier. Whenever anyone needed any menial task done fast, they seemed to yell, "Dusty!"

But Ben didn't know his story. Why was a guy who appeared to be maybe twenty-one or twenty-two doing this work? Did he have aspirations? Goals?

And why the hell do you care?

His phone buzzed on the desk, and he smiled. Well, kind of smiled. "Hi, Alan."

"Hi, dear. What time shall I pick you up?"

Ben stared at the volume of emails that had come in just while he was mooning over a tight ass. *Seriously?* "How about seven?"

"Jesus, Ben, give it a rest. You're the damned head of the foundation."

"Yes, which means I work hardest and longest." Wealthy from birth, Alan Ashland didn't know the meaning of work. Man, what Ben could do with Alan's money in the Clear-Water Foundation, the nonprofit arm of ClearWater Technologies. It could mean clean water. Malaria cures. Alzheimer's protocols. *But damn, I'm lucky to have him.*

The annoyance in Alan's voice vibrated across the phone. "And if you'd get those gorillas out of your house, maybe I could spend the night, at least."

"You can spend the night now. You just have to excuse a little mess." He sighed very quietly.

"'Little mess.' Good God, the construction of the damned pyramids didn't create as much chaos as your so-called renovations."

Okay, his house had exactly one habitable room currently. In Ben's defense, that habitable room was the bedroom, but Alan didn't seem willing to wade through construction workers to get to the bed. Shortsighted of him. Some of those workers were adorable.

Ben snorted. "Come on, Alan. You wouldn't like it if it were as quiet as the Egyptian tombs. You just hate the house."

"Hurry up with your construction. When we get married, you'll get better money for it if it's got a new kitchen and bathrooms."

Right. He *really* wanted to sell his house right after he renovated it. Damn. Ben didn't have time for the same old argument. "I'll see you at seven. Pick me up here."

"Okay."

Ben hung up and set the phone carefully on the desk. Alan was fun—sometimes. And everyone loved him so much. *That includes me, right?*

He glanced up again, but no Dusty. *Good, maybe I'll get some work done.* He wiped a hand over his face. *Right, and maybe I should spend some time working on why a happily engaged man is staring at other guys' butts.*

He settled down to answering the emails, but after about half an hour a tap on the door brought his head up again. "Hey, Craig."

Craig Elson, his VP of marketing, stood in his doorway. "Hi, Ben. Got a minute?"

"Sure. Come on in." Ben sat back, but he couldn't keep his gaze from inspecting the hall and every person who walked by.

"I wanted to go over the advertising strategies for the foundation." Craig followed Ben's glance to the window. "But if you're waiting for someone, I can come back."

"Oh no, sorry. I'm not." He pointed at the round confer-ence table in the corner of his office. "I'd love to see them."

Craig sat and slid his laptop toward Ben, who started scrolling through a series of bullet points on the goals for the campaign—showing corporate America and private donors the brand-building advantages of corporate responsibility. In other words, why they should give money to save whales or cure cancer instead of buying their CEO another beach house.

Craig leaned back in his chair. A tall, nice-looking guy, Craig tended to be on the shy side but was confident in his skills and really excelled at marketing, planning, and analytics. He'd come to the company the previous year, right before Ben had been brought on as VP and executive director of the ClearWater Foundation—the youngest VP in ClearWater's history.

Movement beyond the glass wall of his office caught Ben's eye. He looked up and froze. Dusty was back. This time he slowly bent at the waist as he unwound wires around Mary Kaye's desk. *Dear God.* Ben's face went cold, then hot.

"Uh, Ben?"

"Oh God, Craig I'm sorry. I was just, uh, concerned about the wiring going in at my assistant's desk." He dragged his eyes back to the laptop screen, trying to ignore the little smile tugging at Craig's mouth.

Ben furrowed his brow in forced concentration.

Craig murmured, "He's something, isn't he?"

"What?"

Craig nodded his head toward the window. "Dusty. Like a ray of sunshine captured in a beautiful bottle." He smiled. "He reminds me of my Jesse."

Ben smiled to cover his embarrassment. "Do I know Jesse?"

"Oh right. I forget everyone hasn't met him. My fiancé. Jesse Randall. First time I ever saw him, he was bounding into a coffee shop wearing a T-shirt that proclaimed *I Would Bottom You So Hard.*" Craig shook his head, but the smile on his face spoke of the sweetness of joy. "I was pretty much done for at that moment. He changed my life at every level, like I'd been someone else and suddenly became me." He looked back at the screen. "I'll bet Dusty has that power."

Ben stared at the laptop. "Why do you say that?"

Craig shrugged. "It seems like it would be hard to ever tell him a lie."

Just the idea made Ben swallow a lump in his throat.

"The hardest thing for me was making myself believe I deserved Jesse. I think that's how it is with the special ones." He smiled dreamily.

Ben dragged in a long but silent breath. He pointed at the laptop. "We need to add a reference to the importance of personal recommendation in the Asian community." Maybe if he forced himself to talk about marketing, it would stop him from discussing Dusty Kincaid for the rest of the day, the way he wanted to.

A few minutes later, he managed to not look up when movement in his peripheral vision indicated that Dusty had left the area.

He glanced at Craig. "I didn't realize you were gay."

"Yeah. It's nice to work at a company where that's not a topic of discussion. Actually, it was Jesse who inspired me to apply for the job at ClearWater."

"I'd love to meet him."

Craig nodded. "We should make that happen."

For a second Ben held Craig's gaze. Damn, he wanted to talk. He wanted to spill his guts on... everything, but what the fuck did he have to complain about?

After Craig left, he settled down and worked his ass off until quarter to seven. Then he escaped to the men's room, used his electric razor, brushed his teeth, and practiced smiling. *Show how happy you are to be in this rarified company.*

Fifteen minutes later, he left the lobby and went outside to meet Alan. They'd have to come back for his car, but Alan really liked to pick him up.

Ben sat on the bench beside the entrance, leaned his head against the granite wall, and closed his eyes for a minute. Working hard was his drug of choice. He'd been injected with it at his parents' knees. His mom and dad started with nothing, both of them raised by single parents, if you could call them that—drug addicts who never held a job for more than a few days. All his parents wanted was to have a kid and give him a better life than they had. By the time Ben came along, they'd made a small success and worked even harder to expand it, sending Ben to the best schools, giving him lessons in music, art, tennis, golf—anything that could establish him in a new class of society. They celebrated every one of Ben's successes, but getting engaged to Alan Ashland crowned Ben's achievement in their eyes. He would be a duke to the crown prince of one of the world's richest families.

Ben heard the lobby door open. He sighed and opened his eyes—to a dream.

Earphones plugged in his ears, Dusty sort of danced to the curb, then just kept bobbing and humming to the music only he could hear as he jotted something in a small notebook with a worn pencil.

Ben wanted—what? To go talk to Dusty? But what would he say? *Something. Anything.* Just to make contact. Would the guy think he was nuts? *Oh God—*

A car beeped, and a second later an old, faded silver sedan driven by a woman pulled up to the curb. The door opened, and Dusty hopped in the passenger seat. Just like that, any chance of actually meeting Dusty Kincaid drove away.

Who was that woman? His mother? Maybe even his wife? No, too old.

Again the question arose. Why the hell did he want to know?

Like a reminder from heaven, the rumble of Alan's black Ferrari sounded through the circular drive in front of the ClearWater building, and then the car pulled in front. Ben rose from the bench, walked to the sexy sports car, bent down, and peered inside. He got a shiny smile back. *Wow.* Sometimes he forgot how gorgeous Alan was. The evening sun shone off his pale hair and made his brilliant blue eyes sparkle even more than normal.

Alan leaned across and opened the door, and Ben slid into the low, womblike leather seat that managed to vibrate with the purr of the car, right through his balls.

Alan leaned over and touched Ben's cheek—not a gesture he did often but one Ben loved. Then he pressed his slightly cool, perfectly carved lips to Ben's. When he pulled back, he smiled. "I'm sorry I was such a shit on the phone. Bad day, and I took it out on everyone. I couldn't wait to see you. Highlight of my day."

Well, damn. That was another reminder of why he'd been entranced with Alan to begin with. Charm, sweetness, and all that beauty didn't count for nothing. "I'm happy to see you too. It's been a long day."

Alan pulled away from the curb, some soft rock playing on the sound system. They drove in silence toward the ocean. After a few not totally relaxed minutes, Alan turned down the sound. "I know you love to work, dear, but I hope once we're married you'll let yourself slow down a little." He glanced over and smiled. He must have seen the stiffening in Ben's face, because he said, "Remember you'll be an Ashland. The family's going to need your skills in so many ways. You'll be just as busy, but with different things. More fun things."

Ben smiled and gazed out the window. *Why can nobody get that my work is fun?*

"My folks are so excited about the party." Alan turned into the super exclusive Newport Beach gated community where one of his family homes stared down over the ocean from the cliffs above.

At least on that subject, they could agree. "Mine too. They haven't talked about much else for weeks."

Alan laughed. "My mom's like a kid getting ready for her first date."

Ben chuckled to cover the odd churning in his stomach.

"How was work, Dusty?" As his mom turned left, the old car made that clunking sound again. Dusty Kincaid glanced over in time to see her wince. God, she looked so tired. He needed to find a way to get the car fixed so she didn't have to worry. *Yeah, put that on the list.*

Quit! He took a deep breath and focused his mind on a pink cloud.

She gave him a smile. "You okay?"

"Oh yeah. Great."

"So, work? How was it?"

He felt the smile creep across his face like a little cat.

"That's a good reaction. Did something great happen?"

You mean other than Ben Shane's beautiful smile? "Nothing specific. It's just the people at ClearWater are so nice to me. I really like it there."

"I'm glad, dear. Just be careful not to get overtired."

"I'm careful." He tried not to sound impatient. Nobody wanted more good stuff for him than his mom—even himself.

"Do you have a lot of studying to do tonight?"

"No ma'am."

"Good. We'll eat when we get home and then you can get to bed early. You may like ClearWater but they certainly want you there at the crack of dawn."

Another familiar topic. "I have to be there early or I disturb the people in the offices. You know that."

"Yes, I know." She pulled onto their street, a tract that had seen better days. Except this group of houses had their day somewhere in the last century. Lots of kids played ball in the middle of the road and scampered to the sides as she drove by. A couple boys waved to Dusty. His eyes followed them, maybe still wishing he could have clocked more play time in the street when he was their age.

She parked in the driveway. The garage was so crammed with stuff they saved to take to the swap meet to sell that she couldn't get the car in. She turned to him and smiled as brightly as her tired eyes could manage. "I really am glad you like the job, dear."

He smiled back. She probably wouldn't like the reason he particularly enjoyed this job.

BEN STARED out the window as Alan drove up the street, the too-close-together mansions on the right and the vast darkness of the Pacific on their left, toward the big house with a gazillion lights shining. Cars lined the street, crawling toward valets parking people's expensive vehicles, since even the rich neighborhoods in this area didn't have enough room for more than a few cars.

Alan gave a discreet honk, and one of the valets waved and ran to the gates blocking the driveway. A moment later the gates parted, and Alan managed to maneuver past the cars to turn into the driveway of his parents' home. Alan's home, truthfully. Alan had his own condo in Crystal Cove, but as his parents got older, he spent more and more time living in his suite in the family home. Though just thirty-three, Alan was an only child and therefore the sole inheritor of a vast fortune. Ben's family was comfortable thanks to a buttload of hard work, but the kind of money his father had made paled next to Alan's—a huge, rolling juggernaut of dollars flowing from oil, real estate, and many other self-generating assets.

After turning left in front of the house, Alan ferried the rumbling machine back to the huge garage and parked in front of it. Then he turned to Ben. "Showtime."

"Yes, I guess it is." He smiled.

"In case I forgot to say it, you look lovely tonight."

"Thank you. You too." *So true.* Alan wore a deep blue suit that showed off his fair hair and brilliant eyes perfectly. In deference to California casual, he wore no tie. Likewise, Ben's open-necked white shirt he'd worn all day might be a tad more wilted than Alan's but still passed as party ready with his favorite gray suit. Alan always said it complemented Ben's auburn hair and green eyes.

Alan leaned forward and kissed Ben gently. "That's on account. I'll take you home with me after the party, and then you won't need your car tonight. I can just take you to work in the morning."

Ben bit his tongue. He hated staying at Alan's on work nights. It got him to the office so late the next morning. "Sure. Sounds great."

"Plus we're a little behind on the roll-in-the-hay quotient, so maybe we can make it up. Sound good?"

Ben managed to nod his head with a smile.

Alan climbed out of the car and rounded the front to open Ben's door. He insisted on the gesture although it made Ben feel a little like a 1950s prom queen from Alabama. *Hell, lots of guys would kill for the courtesy.* One more thing that made him feel ungrateful.

With an extended hand, Alan helped him out of the car. The fact that Ben, at nearly six-three, stood four inches taller than Alan likely made this operation look a little silly, but, of course, that might have been why Alan did it. He closed the door behind Ben and slid an arm around his waist. "You're not nervous about this hoopla, are you?"

Ben frowned a little. "No. Should I be?"

"Not at all. It's just that Daddy's invited all his important investors, so he's all over me like diamonds on a debutante to make a good impression."

"But no pressure?" Ben gave him a half smile.

"Right." Alan laughed and led Ben to the back of the house. "Let's sneak in so we can avoid the big meeting-at-the-door scene."

"I'm for that."

The crowd at the front door couldn't be much thicker than the one at the back, but this group was made up of caterers, waiters, bartenders, and one semihysterical coordinator hollering, "What do you mean, the shrimp are still frozen?"

Alan snorted and pulled Ben through the crush to the swinging door that led to the formal dining room. He flashed his teeth at Ben. "Ready?"

"As I'll ever be in this life." For a second Alan gave him an odd look, then threw open the door and stepped through, propelling Ben next to him.

CHAPTER TWO

WHAM. A wall of voices, laughter, glasses clinking, the smells of roast beef and perfume, plus bodies in expensive clothes everywhere—it all hit Ben in the face, and for a second he couldn't catch his breath. Then someone started to clap. Alan swept a bow, then leaned up and gave Ben a kiss. Phone cameras flashed.

Alan's mother, Helen Ashland, looked up from her conversation with two older couples, including Ben's parents. She rushed over to Alan and Ben. "Darlings, making an entrance as usual. You both look simply lovely. Come on, everyone is dying to see you." She stepped between them and took an arm on each side.

With several stops to meet the Ashlands' "very good friend" so and so, or "I'm sure you've heard of" XYZ, Ben finally made it across the dining room to his parents. He gently released himself from Helen's grasp and kissed his mom's cheek. "Having a good time?"

His mom, Mercy Shane, turned overbright eyes on him. "Oh yes. This is the most amazing party." She was dressed in rose-colored lace, a bit overdone for this trendy crowd, but she still looked nice. Her deep auburn hair, green eyes, and striking beauty stood out in any room.

He extended a hand to his father, tall and sturdy, who shook it firmly. "Quite a gathering. Quite a gathering."

As Helen talked to Alan, Ben's mother whispered, "Your father just met the CEO of a company he's been trying to get into for years. The man gave him a card and said to call him tomorrow. The Ashlands certainly know a lot of people." She glanced around. "But then, my God, look at this place. We're so proud of you."

Yeah, look at it. A Mediterranean masterpiece complete with pillars and arched doorways. Alan's apartment resembled it, but it was hard to get anything in Newport that wasn't someone's idea of Mediterranean.

Helen squeezed his arm. "Ben, dear, I'd like you to meet two of our friends, Tiffany Richter and Anastasia Merced." Helen said the latter name like of course he knew who this was, and of course he did. Mother of the family that owned one of the largest retail chains in the world, Anastasia numbered among America's richest women. The Richters weren't even on the same scale. He suppressed a chuckle at his own joke.

"I'm honored, Mrs. Merced. Mrs. Richter." He shook both their hands. From Tiffany he got a loose touching of fingertips, while Anastasia gripped him firmly. She said, "I must say, not many guys can enter the same beauty contest as Alan, but you hold your own just fine. Pleased to meet you, darlin'." Her family home in Arkansas caused her to soften her consonants to nonexistence.

Tiffany Richter looked at Alan, then at Ben. "If anyone had ever told me that I'd be celebrating an engagement between two men, I'd have called them a liar. How times have changed." She shook her head and smiled.

The words fell out of Ben's mouth. "Oh yes, ma'am, you'll find us everywhere these days. Boardrooms, executive suites, the military, courts, on TV, in sports. Look out or your brother might marry one." The shock on his parents' face that he'd said it could only be exceeded by his own.

Alan squeezed his hand—hard—and Ben delivered his most charming smile.

Anastasia threw back her head and blasted... not exactly a laugh. More like a bray. "Tiffany, darlin', that boy just gave you right what you deserve. Say you're sorry and I'll bet he'll do the same."

Alan squeezed again, but Ben just smiled until Tiffany said, "I apologize, Alan and Ben. I didn't mean that the way it sounded."

Ben nodded. "Apology accepted. As you can imagine, the good old days weren't so good for us."

She gazed at him as if this were a revelation. "Well, yes, I suppose that must be true." She looked again at the older and much richer Anastasia. "I really am sorry. That was thoughtless."

"Yes, it was, darlin'. But you'll think better next time." She stuck out her hand to Ben again. "I really am very pleased to meet you. You're some fancy title at ClearWater Tech, am I right?"

Ben shook her hand. "Not fancy, ma'am. I head their nonprofit foundation."

"Oh right, corporate social responsibility?"

"Yes."

"I've been telling my sons that we need to be doing more with our money. Will you have someone call me? I'll see they get to the right one of my sons." She literally reached into her cleavage and brought out a warm, perfumed business card, which she handed to Ben.

"Mrs. Merced, I like your style." He grinned.

"I like yours too, darlin'. Make sure your company knows I gave that card to you." She winked, took Tiffany by the arm, and walked away.

Alan raised an eyebrow. "That seems to be a conquest." He huffed out air. "Could have been a disaster."

Helen looked at Ben sternly. "It certainly could have. Please be more careful, Ben. These are wealthy and influential people. They live in their own bubbles. Just coming to this party is a big step, and many wouldn't have done it except—well, we are the Ashlands."

He took a breath to respond, but the combined pressure of Alan's hand and his parents' worried expressions stopped him. "Yes, ma'am."

Alan gave him a blazing smile. "Excuse us while we get a drink, okay?" He led Ben away from the group.

Ben felt himself tensing. How would Alan react to what he'd said?

As they approached the bar set up in the corner of the great room, Alan said, "Sorry, babe. What a bitch. You should have smacked her."

Ben slowly exhaled as he laughed. If that had been a test—and it had—Alan just passed like a Rhodes scholar in kindergarten. "Thanks, dear. Appreciate that support."

A waiter walked by with a tray of champagne, and Ben snagged one. Alan said, "I'm ready for a scotch. Mind waiting with me?"

"Of course not. There's nowhere I'd rather be." He sipped champagne and controlled the crease that tried to pop between his brows and the tightness that crept into his gut. *Did I just tell a lie?* Couldn't have, no. This was his fiancé. The man he'd chosen to spend his life with. Where else could he possibly prefer to be?

He glanced around at the huge room full of well-dressed people with well-dressed attitudes. In this big-money crowd, his dad—who owned a thriving building maintenance company—was just a highly paid janitor.

As Alan walked back with his glass—being an Ashland had its privileges, so Alan hadn't had to wait—Ben gave his head a little shake.

Alan took his arm. "You okay?"

"Yeah, fine."

"Sadly, since we're the guests of honor, we have to hang around 'til the fat lady sings. So plaster on your best smile, darling, and let's go wow them with their amazing openmindedness for attending a gay engagement party."

Ben laughed. Alan did have a way of saying the right things.

Three semi-miserable hours later, all he could manage to feel was *My face hurts*.

He'd been smiling at things that didn't thrill him, laughing at the nonfunny, and shaking hands with people he never cared to meet again, even though he'd likely meet them again and again after they were married. He was so done. Hell, he could have spent the evening figuring out how to get aid to hurricane victims or curing AIDS.

Ben walked up beside his parents and gave his mom a hug. "We're leaving. Hope you had a wonderful night."

She beamed, but it was all teeth, no eyes. "It's been lovely, dear."

His father gave him the one-armed guy hug. "Quite an evening, son. Congratulations. I hope you'll be as happy as your mother and I have been."

His mother's eyes got shiny. "Thank you, darling." She snuggled against his dad for a minute, and it looked like the old days Ben remembered as a child, with the two of them cuddled on the couch making plans for his future.

A body slammed into his back, and Ben staggered forward, his arm catching the edge of his mother's champagne glass and sloshing it down the front of her dress.

"Oh no." She dabbed at it with her paper napkin.

"Mom, I'm so sorry."

A waiter rushed over with a hand towel.

From behind Ben lurched a woman, expensively dressed in studded leather, her expression perpetually startled from one too many facelifts. She stared up at him with eyes that wouldn't focus. "S-sorry." She grabbed Ben's suit lapels. "Hi. You're the fiancé, right. Didn't mean to run you down. You sure are cute. Too bad you're a fag, right?" She laughed. "I figure I just did the world a favor. I mean, who wants to look at that dress for another hour?" She laughed and stared toward Ben's mother. "Come see me before you go, honey, and I'll tell you where to shop. I mean, jeezuz."

Ben pushed her off him, and she laughed and careened away, almost falling into the middle of a group of people who were chatting by the huge stone fireplace.

Ben stepped to his mom. "I'm sorry, Mom. What a drunken disaster." But he didn't have to look at her long to know the slur had hit right in her gut. She felt uncomfortable with these people, and that bitch had just confirmed that Mrs. Shane didn't belong in this upper-echelon crowd—the crowd she'd worked her whole adult life to be in.

Alan came up beside Ben. "Is everything okay?"

Ben frowned. "No, I—"

His mom slapped on a huge phony smile. "Everything's fine, Alan. Just an unfortunate chain reaction made me spill my champagne, but nothing's lost. I never much liked this dress anyway." Her teeth glistened almost as brightly as the sheen in her eyes. Ben knew damned well she'd probably shopped for three days looking for that dress.

"Oh, I'm sorry." Alan looked from Ben to his mom, obviously knowing something was up, but he didn't push.

It took fifteen more minutes of goodbyes and thank-yous before they made it to Alan's Ferrari. Alan held the door, which inexplicably made Ben want to snap at him that he was a man and could open his own damned door, but he sucked it in and sat in the cushy leather seat, rubbing the bridge of his nose with two fingers.

Alan crawled in the driver's side and glanced at Ben. "I'll bet you're tired after a full day of work. Too bad you couldn't have gotten off early and rested before the party."

Well, shit. "Work energizes me. Making chitchat with two hundred people I don't know is what tires me out. So no, a nap wouldn't have helped."

Silence. Wounded silence.

Double shit.

Ben looked up. "I'm very appreciative of the lovely party your parents gave for us." The words felt like he'd just written *I will not be late to class* five hundred times on a blackboard.

Alan stared out the windshield and drove more slowly, which was an odd tic he always expressed when he was angry. "That was a very expensive party."

"I know."

"They didn't have to do it."

He wanted to scream *I wish they hadn't*, but he bit the inside of his cheek. "I know that too."

"I realize you didn't know anyone and some of those people are a little, uh, uncomfortable with our orientation, but they showed up and they tried."

"Yes. I appreciate that."

"I'm sorry that woman was out of line."

He sighed and didn't cover it. "Alan, I appreciate everything your parents have done for you. But there's an important message here. I love to work. I enjoy the challenge and stimulation of new ideas and problem-solving. I love helping people, communities, countries. I don't love parties. Never have. I tried very hard to be someone you and your family could be proud of tonight, but I'm not a trophy wife or someone who's going to be delighted to entertain your family's business associates night after night. It's not me."

Alan gritted his teeth. "I'm an Ashland. You know what's expected."

"No. I've tried to tell you a bunch of times, I'm not living as your damned hostess."

"I don't want to fight."

Ben softened his voice. "We have to talk about this, Alan. Otherwise we'll end up married with you thinking I'm going to give up most of my work and me thinking you're going to understand that I'll never do that."

"But it's ridiculous, Ben. We have all the money in the world. If I started spending today at top speed, we wouldn't run out before we're dead—or our children are dead."

The word "children" shivered up Ben's back. "I don't do it for money, Alan. I do it because it makes a difference. You know that, and if we had children, I'd want to set them an example of hard work like my dad did for me."

"Your dad sure didn't mind all the contacts he made off the Ashland money tonight."

Give me strength. "Of course. It's exciting to realize a new opportunity and try to move to a new level."

Alan glanced over at Ben with a frown. "Then I'll throw that back at you. How much fun will it be when your work doesn't matter one whit? When your salary is pocket change?"

"Maybe I'll run for office, build a new green city, or invest in new treatments that cure some disease and give them away. I'll never stop working. It's what I love."

They pulled up to a stoplight in silence. Alan's voice was small. "I thought you loved me."

Ben's hand's hit the dashboard. "Damn it, Alan. Love goes both ways. You can't love me and not like anything about me. I try to be engaged in whatever interests you, but beyond tennis, trips to the gym, and lying on the beach, I don't know what that is."

The light changed, and Alan drove through the intersection with his jaw muscle jumping. He took a long slow breath. "You're right."

"What?"

"I say I love your vision and intelligence and commitment, and then I ask you to act like my, what did you call it? A trophy wife? I'm sorry. We'll figure out a way to make this work." Alan grasped Ben's hand and squeezed.

Ben sucked a slow breath. They'd had this conversation at least a dozen times, usually ending in some variation of the speech Alan had just given. He always meant it—until he forgot.

Alan turned left toward his Crystal Cove community. It was upscale and more than a bit pretentious. Ben's renegade mind added the words *Kind of like Alan.*

Suddenly his belly clenched and his lungs felt too big for his chest. "Alan, I need to go home."

"What? But we said—"

"No, *you* said. I'm sorry, but I've got a really early meeting, and you know how you hate to get up at six or earlier. I need to be home with my car, so drop me at the office and I'll see you Friday." The Ashlands had insisted on having the engagement party on Wednesday night since it was a good night for their friends to attend. The rich and famous all went away on the weekends.

Alan turned the wheel and performed a screeching-tire U-turn in the middle of the street, cutting off a minivan struggling up the hill.

"Fuck, Alan." Ben grabbed the dashboard, pulling hard against his seat belt.

"Sorry. I passed the turn." But his knuckles shone white against the steering wheel.

Five minutes later, Ben kissed Alan's cheek, climbed out of the car in the parking lot behind ClearWater, and watched the Ferrari pull away in an automotive version of righteous indignation. His mind pulled in two ways. Alan had a right to be angry, and, if ever there was proof of the lie that they would "work something out," he might have just seen it. God, why did every date, practically every conversation, end with Ben weighing if Alan was the right man for him? Ben wanted to care for Alan. *Why can't I get there? Why does everyone else want me to love Alan more than I want to? Damn.*

CHAPTER THREE

A HALF hour later, Ben parked his hybrid Lexus in his garage behind the cottage and walked into the partly demolished kitchen. Admittedly, the renovations were taking longer than he wanted, but his lack of time meant he didn't supervise the work as closely as he needed to. The contractor he'd used was someone Alan recommended, and the guy was overcommitted —to everything except Ben's renovation, it seemed.

Still, no place like home, as one of his favorite childhood movies said. He was in the process of knocking down a few walls to give the house more open sightlines, but it still retained that Laguna cottage charm, with old hardwood on the floors, big picture-style windows, a backyard full of trees, and a gazebo that conjured romance novels. Plus he had a whole guest cottage out there that he'd start renovating as soon as he finished the house. The house had been an amazing find, a great investment, and, most important, he loved the place. *Sell it, my ass.*

He walked back to his bedroom, the one place currently unsullied by demolition madness, and undressed in his big closet—big because he'd turned one of the small bedrooms into a dressing room. Yes, thank you, he was gay. Wearing pajama bottoms and nothing else, he scooted on his flip-flops to keep nails and drywall dust off his feet and went to the kitchen for a big glass of water and a piece of string cheese. Dear God, every hors d'oeuvre at the party seemed to have a minimum of four ingredients, none of which appeared to go together. *Bacon and peanut butter? Seriously?*

He leaned his butt against the counter and peeled the plastic on the cheese. *What in the hell am I doing?* Alan had swept him off his feet eleven months before at a friend's wedding reception. He'd hovered on Ben's every word and professed to admire his work and dedication. To celebrate their three-month anniversary, he'd taken Ben to Paris, and they'd toured museums and walked hand-in-hand beside the Seine. When Ben wanted to visit French hospitals and schools, Alan had set it up for them. But things started to change. Vacation trips became frequent visits to a string of virtually identical white sand beaches, and Alan needed more and more of Ben's time for dinners with family friends and essential parties at their home in Palm Beach, Newport, St. John, or Aspen. *We'll just take the plane. We'll only be gone a couple of days.* Ben's work got lower on the priority list while his wardrobe and hairstyle came under closer scrutiny.

But there was a warmth and charm to Alan that Ben had originally fallen in love with. He seemed torn between being an Ashland and honestly wanting to make a difference in the world. And Ben's parents thought they'd died and gone to heaven. The engagement was the culmination of their dreams for him.

He sighed, tossed the plastic in the recycle bin, grabbed his water, and headed for the bedroom again. *Why can't I settle down and just be grateful? How hard is it to be that rich?*

No time to think about it tonight. I'll think some more tomorrow.

He crawled in bed, flipped off the light, and closed his eyes. *Right, Scarlett O'Hara. You do that.*

Ben yawned hugely as he unlocked his office door. Yes, it was early—5:30 a.m.—but it wasn't the time that made his eyelids heavy. It was staring at the damned ceiling, picking petals off daisies, chanting *I love him. I love him not.*

Not totally accurate. I do love him. I mean, I think.

Shit. He crossed to his desk, flipped on his computer as he took off his suit jacket, and hung it over his chair back. He needed to get some research done before his meeting with his staff at 7:00 a.m. Settling in his chair, he took a deep breath, cleared his mind, and got to work.

He was deep in analysis of the testing on training of therapy dogs when a bang against the wall made him look up.

Dusty Kincaid stood outside the office door clutching a wastepaper basket and staring at Ben with wide eyes but a big smile. "I'm so sorry, Mr. Shane. The trash can got away from me."

"Not a problem, uh, Dusty. Just startled me is all." He glanced at the clock—6:15 a.m. "You're here early."

"I like to get a jump on things, sir."

Ben smiled. Dusty had a musical voice—kind of high and dancing. Ben wanted to hear it again. "What's on your agenda today?"

"Well, I have to get the trash emptied into the main can so the cleaning service can take it out. I do that so strangers aren't walking into the offices. Too much valuable stuff in them. May I take yours, Mr. Shane?"

"No, that's okay. I'll dump it later. I'll just end up filling it again." He chuckled. "I guess I make a lot of mistakes."

"I doubt that, sir."

Something in Dusty's big blue eyes made Ben's heart slam against his ribs. A couple of smile lines suggested he might not be quite as young as he seemed. Maybe more like twenties rather than teens. Ben swallowed hard. "So, uh, what else are you doing today?"

Dusty clutched the trash can against his chest and ran his other hand through his chin-length golden hair. "They have some shelves that need building in the lunchroom, so I've got to get to work on that."

"Oh, you build things?"

"Yes. That's what I did before I started work at ClearWater, but I really like it here better."

Ben cocked his head. "So you worked for a builder?"

"Yes, sir. Carpentry and stuff. Some things I can't do, but most I can." He glanced at the clock on the wall. "I better get to work. Sure is nice talking to you." He smiled almost shyly.

"Yes. You too."

Dusty turned and walked into Mary Kaye's cubicle, set the trash can under her desk, then turned.

Ben's brain threw out an idea before his mouth could resist. "Uh, Dusty."

God, those teeth must be lighted from inside. "Yes, sir?"

"Would you ever consider doing some construction supervision?"

He shook his head, the golden hair rippling. "Oh no, sir, I'm not qualified. That takes real expertise."

"No, no. I don't mean like that. I mean checking on a crew of construction guys and keeping them on track."

Dusty cocked his head quite seriously. "That might be

something I could do. Why? Do you need help? I'd be happy to help you."

Jesus, what are you thinking? But his insides felt like they'd turned to pudding—sweet, soft, and melty. Ben shrugged. "I'm not sure. What hours do you work here?"

"I work three days a week, part-time."

"Are you busy on the other days?"

"Yes, I go to school."

"Oh." Ben smiled. "That's great."

"I think so too." He waited expectantly.

"Well, maybe I could—uh, maybe I can contact you and set something up." *What are you saying?* "I mean, maybe I can arrange times for you to help at my house—where they're renovating." Holy hell, did he have any more feet to shove in his mouth?

"Where do you live?"

"Laguna Beach."

A crease flashed between his brows. "It's a little hard to get there. But I'm sure I can figure out the schedule."

"Yes, we're going into summer and the traffic is really bad, but if you come at the right hours, it shouldn't be hard. I'll be glad to pay your fee to include driving time."

"That wouldn't be fair, sir. The bus takes too long. But I'm sure we can work something out."

Dusty being picked up in front of the building flashed in Ben's mind. "Oh, you don't have a car."

Dusty walked to Ben's desk and took hold of a pen, then glanced around. Ben shoved a pad of paper at him. Dusty wrote a phone number on the lined pad, then flashed that dimpled wonder of a smile. "No, I don't. Please call me if I can help." He turned and left the office.

How could one simple conversation leave him feeling shell-shocked?

Ben gathered up some reports and went to his meeting. When he came back an hour later, Mary Kaye, his admin, sat at her desk. "Hey, Ben. How was your engagement party?"

"Great, thanks." He pulled his business card case from his breast pocket and fished out Anastasia Merced's card. With a grin, he handed it to Mary Kaye. "Looky who I met last night."

"Woo-hoo! Man, get engaged every night."

He cringed a little but tried not to show it.

"This is serious money. But is she seriously interested in giving us some of it?" She laughed.

"I think so. She said to have someone call her. I think that someone is me."

"Want me to get her on the phone?"

"Yeah. Give me a few minutes to research their current contributions."

"I'll do some digging too. Just yell when you want me to call."

Ben nodded and turned toward the office—then stopped. "Uh, Mary Kaye, what can you tell me about Dusty?"

"Our Dusty? Kincaid?"

He nodded.

She shrugged. "Sweet as an angel, reliable. Never misses a day. I think he's a college student. No idea in what. Funny. Everyone really likes him, but I realize not many people know too much about him. At least I don't. You could ask HR. Why? Is there a problem?"

"Oh no. You know how I complain that the construction guys who're renovating my house don't get much done because their supervisor leaves for another job and there's no one to keep them working? I was thinking I could have Dusty go over with a to-do list a few times a week, and if they knew he was from me, they might do what he says."

"You think? He's capable, but he's such a sweetie, I can't imagine a bunch of hammer jockeys paying much attention to him."

"Yeah. Maybe not." *Get over your stupidity. Go back to work.*

After discovering that the Merced companies paid out a tiny percentage of their profits to charity, he asked Mary Kaye to make the call. A couple of minutes later, she buzzed him. He took a deep breath and picked up the phone. "Mrs. Merced."

"Anastasia, darlin'."

"And I'm Ben, or better yet, darlin'."

She laughed as he'd hoped. She said, "Now I'm guessing that you've already done your homework, and you're calling to chastise me for the meager pittance we give to charity."

"I wasn't going to bring that up."

"Like fudge you weren't. And it's high time we did something about it. So why don't I set up a dinner at my house with my sons, and you do a presentation of the many charities we could become involved in through the ClearWater Foundation. You can bring that handsome fiancé of yours if you want."

"You sure they won't mind mixing business with their pleasure?"

"That's their favorite kind of business, darlin'. And Mama's dinners are a command performance."

Whew. He could well imagine. Still, tying a large potential donor with his personal life made him... uneasy. Maybe because his personal life felt uneasy. "Just let me know when."

"I'll call you to set it up."

"I'm looking forward to it." He hung up. Just the thought

of how Alan would lord this over him made him cringe. He could hear it. *See how valuable the Ashland name is?*

He stood. *Don't be petty.*

Mary Kaye stuck her head in the door. "How'd it go?"

"Great. She's setting up a dinner with her sons."

"Holy shit—excuse me."

"Second the motion."

They both grinned. This could be a big win for the foundation. He plunged back into a program he was working on until Mary Kaye stuck her head in the door again. "It's past lunchtime. Want me to get you something from the cafeteria?"

"No, I'll walk with you and see what looks good to me."

Five minutes later, he knew exactly what looked good to him. Yes, there was a chance he hadn't understood that Dusty was going to be working in the cafeteria. Now he knew.

No one was building the shelves right then. In fact, Dusty sat on the floor beside a pile of lumber leaning against the wall with a set of earphones on, eyes closed and lips moving slightly. He looked—serene. Peaceful. Like if you got close, you could soak it up from his pores.

Mary Kaye said softly, "I see him doing that sometimes. Sweet, isn't it?"

"Yeah, it's like he's meditating."

"I think he is." She looked toward the food-service counter. "Come on before they close."

Ben dragged his eyes away from the beautiful Dusty to look at the menu. Mary Kaye got a chef's salad, and Ben ordered fish and chips. She said, "Want to take it back to the office or eat here?"

"Uh, here's good."

Her eyes flicked toward Dusty, who'd left his seated

posture and was measuring boards, and she smiled. They carried their food to a table in the middle of the room.

By the time they'd chatted their way through about half their lunch, most of the people in the room were gone, the service was shutting down the hot food line, and Dusty balanced lumber in an effort to get it into place. He glanced toward the door a couple of times with that crease between his golden eyebrows Ben had observed earlier.

As Ben and Mary Kaye dumped their trash, a young guy, sloppily dressed, sauntered through the door to the lunchroom. Dusty walked firmly over to him. "Hey, man, you were supposed to be here half an hour ago."

The guy shrugged. "No big. Who cares? We'll get it done."

Dusty had to look up to the big guy, but he still got in his face. "If you want this job, you'll be on time and work hard or we'll find someone else. You got that?"

"Who made you my boss?"

"The company, that's who. So do you want to work or do you want to leave the way you came?"

The dude held up his hands. "Sorry. I want to work."

"Then let's get to it." Dusty turned and stalked over to the lumber. "Take that end."

Mary Kaye stared at Ben and widened her eyes. As they walked out of the cafeteria, Dusty and his minion were working hard.

In the hall she said, "Dayum, who knew that sweet boy could be such a taskmaster?"

"Yeah." Just exactly what he needed.

CHAPTER FOUR

———

"Good night, Ben."

Ben looked up at Mary Kaye. "Night. See you tomorrow."

"Right. Friday. Why don't you consider taking a weekend off for a change?"

"There's so much construction at my house, it's quieter here." He leaned back. "But I have a date for Friday night."

"With your fiancé?"

"Who else?"

"See you." She waved as she walked toward the elevator.

Ben gave her enough time to leave the floor, then got up, walked to the door of his office, and looked out. Things had quieted. Most of the company was high-tech—the foundation was just a small subsidiary of do-gooding—and tech people worked at all hours, so a few still clicked away. But Thursday night was a popular meat-market evening at the local bars, and the attraction of beer and possible hookups trumped even the compulsion to overwork.

What about Dusty?

Ben hurried toward the cafeteria and smiled when he saw Dusty walking quickly toward him. The worn denim pulled tightly across his thigh muscles and his fair hair bounced as he moved. *Wow.*

Ben said, "Hi. I was just coming to find you."

"Me?" His dimples popped all over his face.

"Yes, uh, I wanted to ask you about doing that work at my house."

"Oh. Yes, sir. I want to. It's just that"—he glanced toward the elevator—"the last bus is leaving, and if I miss it, I can't get home. Could we talk on the phone? Or I could come in tomorrow, or—"

"Can I drive you home, Dusty?"

"Oh." His eyes widened. "That would be a lot of trouble."

Ben smiled. "Not unless you live in Nevada."

"What? Oh no. Anaheim." Then his sweet face burst into a shy smile, and his cheeks flushed. "Sorry. Thank you. I'd love a ride."

Ben led the way to his car in the side parking lot. Despite some urge to open the door for Dusty, he resisted and slid into the driver seat. When Dusty was buckled in beside him, Ben turned on some Chopin, playing very softly, and said. "Give me the address for the GPS."

Dusty rattled off a number, and they took off.

Ben said, "What I'd like you to do is come to my house and check the work of the crew before they leave. Since you have building experience, you'll know if they're accomplishing what's on the to-do list. What hours do you have available?"

"I work at ClearWater Monday and Wednesday and sometimes Thursday, like today. I go to school Monday night and Tuesday and Friday in the morning."

"What are you studying?"

"Computer programming."

"That's really useful." Ben turned onto the freeway and headed north.

"And philosophy."

"What?" Ben looked over quickly, then back at the road as he merged into the midevening traffic. "Unusual combination."

"Yes, it's stimulating and soothing. I like knowing that others have asked the same questions I do."

For a second Ben couldn't catch his breath. "Is there some time you might be able to work for me?"

"Sure. Construction guys usually start early, so sometimes I might be able to come before work or school, and other days after."

"If you come early, I can take you to work with me."

"That'd be great. Get off at the next exit."

Ben pulled off and drove down Katella. The big signs showed the way to the parking lots for Disneyland. "Do you like living near the Magic Kingdom?"

"Oh, I guess. It means there are lots of buses."

"What's your favorite ride?" The bright lights came up on the right.

"Not sure."

"I know, there are so many fantastic attractions, right? Like the Jungle Cruise. Have you been on Soarin' at California Adventure?"

"Is it great? Turn right up here."

"Uh, yes." He turned. "It's like flying."

"Right again, then follow the road around."

"Haven't you ever been on Soarin?"

"Never been to Disneyland." Dusty stared through the windshield.

"Really?" Ben looked around the shabby neighborhood.

"It's the house at the end of the cul-de-sac on the left."

The house was practically falling down, but the yard was neatly cut, and a few plants blossomed in front of the rickety-looking porch. No lights were on.

"Do you live alone?" Ben peered through the side window.

"My mom's a nurse. Sometimes she works nights."

"Oh, you live with your mother?" *Maybe he is as young as he looks.*

"Yes, it's best." He opened the car door. "Thank you, sir. When would you like me to start?"

"Uh, first, since we're going to be colleagues, how about you call me Ben?"

"Okay." He beamed.

"And you tell me when you can be there."

"Tomorrow morning?"

"Yes, great."

"Will you text me the address?"

Ben nodded and pulled out his phone.

"Thank you again. Drive safely." He climbed out, slammed the door, and walked with his signature bounce to the entrance of the broken-down house. With Dusty at the door, the ugly place might have been Cinderella's Castle.

"Morning, Ben." Artie, the plumber, stuck his head out from under the new apron sink and waved a wrench at Ben.

Ben nodded and made some kind of welcoming sound as he staggered toward the already steaming coffee maker, scratching his bare chest. He'd managed to slide on his flip-flops against the nails and splinters, but delaying coffee long enough to throw on a T-shirt was asking too much.

He filled his favorite mug with french roast, loaded it with half-and-half from the carton in the dusty but still-working fridge, then blew on the mixture for a second before sucking in a slow, long mouthful. *Bliss.*

Two other guys, one of whom Ben didn't recognize, walked through the kitchen on their way to the sunporch. "Morning."

"Morning."

"There's some guy looking for you on the front porch."

"What?" Sloshing his coffee, he hurried across the kitchen, flip-flopped through what had been the old-fashioned living room and dining room and was now becoming one great room, and got to the screen door. Dusty stood on the porch in clean Levis and a long-sleeved blue T-shirt that brought out the sky of his eyes. "Hi."

"Hi, sir, uh, Ben. The bus didn't take long." Ben held the screen door open, and Dusty walked through into the house. He seemed to glance at Ben's bare chest, and his eyes ricocheted away. His head made a big circle. "Wow. This is nice."

"I hope it will be."

"No. It is now, and it'll be even better. These are really good ideas."

Ben said, "By the way, we didn't discuss your payment. Since you'll be doing supervisory work, I think I should increase the hourly rate you're paid at ClearWater."

Dusty shook his head. "Oh no, they're more than generous. That will be fine." He stepped in the middle of the room and frowned at a laminated beam sitting on the floor. "Has anyone verified that this beam is big enough to do the job?" He looked up. "That's a long expanse."

"Uh, how would I find out?"

"You must have used an architect, right? He should have specified the size of the beam based on what the structural engineer said. He'd have to do that to get a permit."

"So it should be on the plans?"

"Yes, sir. Ben."

"Uh, my builder has the plans, but I think I've got a copy."

"It'd be good to have a set I can check." Dusty walked through the open space, looking around with interest, smiling. "I love these ideas." He pulled a notebook out of his pocket and jotted some things down.

"You like to take notes?"

He nodded as he wrote. "It helps me remember."

"I'll look for the plans." Dusty didn't waste any time. Ben walked down the hall to his home office, dug around in the binder he kept of papers associated with the remodel, and found his copy of the plans. After pulling them out, he hurried back to the great room, but no Dusty. He heard voices from the partly open kitchen and followed them.

Dusty stood with his notebook open. He was saying, "Good to meet you, Artie. Sam. Ben's going to give all his notes to me, and I'll bring them and coordinate with you. So I'll be back this afternoon by three. I want to talk to you two and whoever else is working with you to go over all the priorities, okay?"

Artie frowned. "Uh, we got a supervisor. Bruce works for our boss."

Dusty smiled sweetly. "Right, but he's got a lot of jobs. You guys have this one. Me too. So you'll report in to Mr. Shane by way of me." He looked up. "Any questions?"

The two guys glanced at Ben, then shook their heads.

Dusty grinned at him, dimples flashing. "Hi, Ben. Ready to go over your to-dos for the day?"

"How about you look at the plans while I dress and then we can discuss it with Artie and—"

Dusty glanced at his notebook. "Sam."

"Right. Sam." He handed the plans to Dusty and escaped back to the relative quiet and order of his bathroom. He'd renovated it when he turned the extra bedroom into a dressing room the year before. With a twist of the faucet, he revved up the hot water, stripped, and stepped under the waterfall flow —one of the indulgences he'd built into his house. Grabbing his razor, he went to work. No, he wouldn't think about Dusty in his shower. Most of all, he wouldn't think about being in his shower with Dusty.

He plopped his butt against the slate wall—the cold slate wall—and backed away fast. *I shouldn't be thinking about Dusty in any capacity except a construction helper.* Jesus, he might be too young, and even if he was thirty, Ben had no reason to think the guy was gay. *Shit, and I'm engaged!* He slapped a hand against the wall. *What's wrong with me?*

He rinsed, turned off the water, dried, and dressed without further pornographic musings. Fastening his belt as he walked, he went back to the great room and found Dusty leaning over the plans. Ben said, "See anything important?"

Dusty looked up with that sweet smile that made Ben's heart flip. "Yes. The guys agree that this lam beam isn't to spec. Someone must have misread it. They've called their supervisor, and I'll check it this evening."

"Man, thanks, Dusty. You've already more than justified my decision to hire you."

"I'm really glad."

Ben fished in his pants pocket. "Here's a key to the house in case you need to come in when I'm not here."

Dusty looked like he'd been given the crown jewels. "Thank you. I'll be very careful with it." He wrote a note on his lined page.

Ben nodded. "I know you will. Can I drop you at school on my way to work?"

"Yes, thanks. That would be great."

Dusty hurried into the kitchen and reminded the workers that he'd be back, then trotted to Ben. "Ready."

In the car Dusty said, "Can we listen to that nice music again?"

He'd noticed. "Sure." Ben flipped on the Chopin.

For a few minutes, they rode in music. Ben cleared his throat. "Dusty, do you mind if I ask how old you are?"

"Oh sure. I'm twenty-three. How old are you?"

Ben almost laughed. As an executive in a top firm, nobody ever asked him that. But turnabout was fair. "I'm twenty-nine."

"Wow. You've done a lot in your life."

"Thank you." Ben glanced at Dusty.

"I haven't been able to do so much, but I'm working at it."

"That's what counts. Keep moving toward your dreams."

"I like that idea a lot." He leaned his head back and closed his eyes.

"So your dad doesn't live at home?"

"No. Never has. My mom's taken good care of me, though."

"Has she always been a nurse?"

"No. She had to work so hard. She was only sixteen when she had me, but she never gave me up, no matter what anyone said." He took a deep breath and let it out in a long exhale. "And no matter how hard it was."

"She sounds amazing."

"She is." He looked out the window. "It's hard for her to, you know, let me do stuff, but she's the best mom."

"So you're not married?" Ben chuckled.

Dusty mirrored the chuckle. "Not yet."

"Have a girlfriend?" *Oh, very subtle, Shane.*

"No."

"Not yet, huh."

"Not ever. I'm gay. But I don't have a boyfriend yet. I'd like to, though."

Well, okay. Ben swallowed. "You would?"

"Sure, wouldn't you?"

"I'm, uh, engaged." *Shit. Shit. Shit. When did I decide to become Mr. Purveyor of Truth?*

The passenger seat became deeply silent.

Ben glanced over. Dusty's eyes were closed, and he seemed to be breathing deeply.

"You okay?"

"What?" His eyes fluttered open.

"Sorry. Just asking how you're doing?"

"Good, thanks. Just drop me on the curb over there." He pointed to one of the entrances to Orange Coast College.

"How will you get back to my place?"

"Bus." He smiled, but his glance scampered all over the place as he opened the door. "Have a great day."

Ben couldn't stop. He put a hand on Dusty's arm—his sinewy, muscled, hot-as-fuck arm. "Dusty, what's wrong? Come on, tell me."

"Nothing, honest. Just sometimes it's hard not to wish I was somebody else." He finally met Ben's gaze with his own, the deep blue as stormy as a hurricane in the Caribbean. "Bye." He was out of the car and walking toward the campus, while Ben tried hard not to stare at his beautiful butt.

With a sigh Ben headed toward work. Something about Dusty made him uneasy. Something was missing. Something Ben didn't know. Twenty-three, but he lived at home. Okay, so he might have an overprotective mom whom he felt he owed a lot so he didn't leave, or maybe he was a fuckup in his teens and now he stayed with his mom to get back on his feet, or— *Jesus. I don't need to know.*

His phone buzzed. One more sigh. "Answer."

"Ben?"

"Hi, Alan."

"What would you like to do tonight?"

Oh. "Maybe a quiet dinner, you and me?"

"Sounds great. Shall I pick you up?"

What the hell? "Sure."

"That's great. We'll catch some dinner, and then my folks are meeting some clients for drinks. I told them we'd stop by."

The third sigh was long and very quiet.

CHAPTER FIVE

Dusty hurried up the street toward Ben's house. *Such a pretty neighborhood.* He sure would like to have a place like this for his mom to live—someday. *Stop. All's well. It's as it should be.* He tried to breathe deeply and slowly, but he kept tightening his chest.

His brain felt... wired. Not good. But the very slight chance he might see Ben made him want to rush. Just knowing he got to do something for Ben filled him with fizz. Also not good. The edges of his vision wiggled.

He stopped and took three deep breaths. *Calm down.*

Feeling a little more serene, he started walking again and made it to Ben's house plenty fast enough. When he got inside, Artie and Sam both sat leaning against the wall in the kitchen, smoking.

Dusty backed up and waved a hand. "Hey, if you've got to smoke, go in the backyard. That smell never comes out."

Artie frowned and Sam made a growly sound, but they walked to the back door and threw out their half-finished smokes.

Dusty examined the lam beam. He looked at the two

guys. "This looks right."

Artie nodded. "Yeah. Our boss said he just had the wrong one brought over."

Dusty looked straight into the guy's eyes. "It's a good thing we found it, right? Since Mr. Shane is paying for this size beam. And the plans specify this beam."

"Yeah. A good thing." He stood. "So we're done for the day."

"As soon as I check the work, okay? That's what Mr. Shane wants."

"Oh yeah, right."

Dusty began a slow walk around the house, checking the jobs the guys said they'd have done that day. Most were completed. He pointed out a couple of details, got agreement from Artie to work on them the next day, and Dusty wrote them in his notebook.

Artie and Sam left, pulling away in their truck. Dusty put his checklist on the new, granite, very grimy but very pretty kitchen island, then ripped a page from his book to write a note to Ben. He glanced through the window into the back-yard. *Wow*.

Slowly he walked out the door from the kitchen onto a small porch overlooking the slightly overgrown wonderland. The trees created a canopy over part of the yard, so it made him want to lean against a tree trunk and read or just dream. The detached garage stood on one side, but at the back was a freestanding building.

He hopped off the porch and crossed the grass, then peered in the window. A house. Small, but a house. He rounded the building to the front door and tried the knob. It opened and he grinned, peeking inside. *So cool*. He stood in a medium-sized room with a kitchen on one side and lots of windows looking out into the yard. He wandered down a small hall and discovered a bathroom and a good-sized bedroom. It must be a guest cottage. It needed work, but not that much. Maybe new fixtures and appliances, but the basic structure was there. His hands twitched. It would be so fun to fix up this place. *Imagine having a cozy spot like this?*

Quit snooping. He left the cottage and returned to the kitchen. He glanced at his note to Ben to be sure he hadn't missed anything and then slid it back on the kitchen island.

A knock on the front door made him look toward it. For a second his heart leaped. *Ben! No, silly, why would he knock on his own door?*

Should I answer it? Not my house.

He half-shrugged, took a breath, walked to the door, and opened it with what he hoped was a polite and professional expression. A beautiful blond man stood outside. The guy raised an eyebrow at Dusty. "Who are you?"

Okay, not a very polite and professional greeting. "I work for Mr. Shane. Can I help you?"

"Work for him doing what?"

"Excuse me, but who are you?"

He planted a fist on his hip. "I'm *Mr.* Shane's fiancé, and I'm wondering what you're doing in his house."

Oh dear. His heart beat hard. Too hard. He drew in a slow breath. "I'm sorry. I'm Dusty. I'm supervising the work being done on Mr. Shane's house when he's not able to be here."

"I see." The man pushed past Dusty into the entry, then walked straight to the great room.

Dusty followed and found him staring around, shaking his head, and looking kind of disgusted.

"Is there a problem, sir?"

"Oh dear God, in one day I've become a sir. What are you, a teenager?"

"No, sir. But I don't know your name."

"I'm Alan Ashland. You say your name's Dusty?"

"Yes."

"Well, Dusty, can you tell me how a grown man of relatively good taste can bear to live in this pigsty when he could stay with me in a perfectly beautiful and clean townhouse?"

"I think he likes this house, Alan."

"Jesus! As somebody famous said, 'What a dump.'"

"Bette Davis, and I don't think this is a dump. This is a beautiful house that reflects Ben's taste."

"Oh, he's Ben now."

Dusty frowned. "He asked me to call him Ben."

"Where did he find you?" That statement didn't have a pleasant sound, and Dusty's hands clenched—never a good sign.

"I work with him at ClearWater."

Alan laughed derisively. "Right. You must be the VP of marketing."

The voice came from the half-finished doorway between the kitchen and the service porch. "Dusty's my construction supervisor, Alan. Is there some kind of problem?"

Dusty's first instinct was to apologize and run out the door, but an edge to Ben's voice might mean he wasn't mad at Dusty. More likely he was mad at his fiancé—which made Dusty want to smile—which wasn't nice.

Alan waved a hand. "No, no, dear. No problem. I was just surprised to find a stranger in your house."

"He's not a stranger to me."

"I understand. It must be very reassuring to have someone to help with this never-ending project."

Wow. Alan sure doesn't like Ben's house.

Alan put a hand on Ben's arm. "Are you close to ready?" He looked at Ben's suit with a little attitude.

"Yeah, sorry. I got caught in a meeting." Ben turned to

Dusty. "Is there anything important I should know?"

Dusty pointed at the note and his checklist. "I think it's all there."

Ben picked up the list even though Alan glanced at his expensive watch. Ben said, "This is great. So they replaced the beam."

"Yes. You need to keep an eye on their boss. If he'd put in the wrong beam, you would likely not have passed inspection, and it would've cost a lot."

"Great catch, Dusty." He looked up and their eyes met, which made Dusty shiver. "How are you getting home?"

"Bus."

"I'd be happy to loan you my car if you can bring it back tomorrow."

Alan's eyes got wide. "You what?"

"Dusty doesn't have a car. He can borrow mine."

The guy couldn't close his mouth.

Dusty held up a hand. "Thank you, but I can't drive. The bus doesn't take too long."

Ben frowned. "We can drive you home."

Alan practically blew steam out of his ears like in an old cartoon. "We don't have time for that. I made reservations—"

"I like the bus." Dusty purposefully gave Alan a big pretend smile. "Thank you, though." He looked back at Ben. "Do you need me tomorrow? I don't have class or work in the morning."

A line showed up between Ben's eyebrows. "If you wouldn't mind, the contractors will be here tomorrow morning and, uh, I'll be gone. It would be a big help if you could check in on them whenever works for you."

"That would be fine. I'll be here." Dusty glanced at his sneakers. "Have a good night."

Hurrying, he walked to the door and out into the cool

evening. When he got to the sidewalk, he broke into a jog. The bus would be at the stop in five minutes. He felt weirdly of two minds again—happy he could do something else to help Ben tomorrow, and sad because Ben couldn't supervise the contractors himself.

Oh, Dusty. What in hell are you doing?

COME ON. *Come on.*

Ben sat at the distressed wood, pseudo-Mediterranean island in Alan's kitchen, sipping coffee and trying not to look at his watch.

Alan sailed in, adjusting the sweater he'd tied casually around his shoulders, kissed Ben on the cheek, and poured himself a cup of coffee that he whitened with his favorite vanilla-flavored creamer. *Yuk.* "You were sure up and at 'em this morning. Obviously I didn't tire you out enough last night. Are you ready for another round? Maybe you'll actually relax." He flashed his lascivious grin.

Ben smiled back and raised the coffee cup to his mouth in case it looked phony. *This is not good. I'm being a miserable pretender and I hate it.* Everything in him screamed to tell Alan that he didn't want another round because he hadn't enjoyed the last one. He kept hoping he'd develop some chemistry with the man he said he loved. It used to be that he just felt kind of blah after sex, but he thought he was tired, stressed, anything to explain it. Last night had reached a new low. When Alan touched him, his skin almost crawled. He wanted to slide out of the bed and call a cab.

Why didn't you?

He got up and poured a little more coffee.

Alan said, "So Mommy and Daddy would love us to join them at the club for brunch. Want to go?"

"Oh, that's nice of them, but I need to get home, check on the contactors, and then head over to the office."

"Shit, Ben! It's fucking Saturday. Can't you give it up for a damned minute?"

Everything in Ben froze. He reached in his pocket, pulled out his phone and clicked the Uber icon, input Alan's address, drank the last of his coffee slowly while Alan stared at him like he was an idiot, and walked to the bedroom for his stuff. Loading his clothes from the previous night into his tote, he crossed from the bedroom to the front door and out.

"What the hell?" Alan yelled behind him.

Striding down the pathway from Alan's condo toward the street, he waved a hand at the driver, and then leaned over. "You got here fast. Thanks."

"I was just down the street." The driver looked over Ben's shoulder, and his eyes widened.

Ben looked up as Alan ran down the path barefoot. "Where are you going?"

"Home to get my car."

"Don't be this way." He half smiled.

"Listen, dear, when you say that, what I hear is you want me to be some way other than who I am. I'm sorry. I can't do that."

"Of course I don't mean that. I'm just disappointed not to get to spend the day with you, that's all."

"I told you last night I had to go to work this morning. You agreed, and yet you made plans with your parents that included me."

Alan stared at the ground, arms tightly crossed.

Ben opened the car door. "This way you can have brunch with your folks and I can get my work done. We'll talk later." He slid in, closed the door, and nodded to the apprehensive driver, who drove away with dispatch.

"You guys break up?"

"Not exactly. Just a disagreement."

"You want to work and he wants to have brunch?" He snorted. "Sounds like me and my wife."

"Yeah. The universal argument, gay or straight." Ben laughed and leaned back. *Why didn't I stay and have a serious talk with Alan? He seemed willing to compromise to try to save the relationship.*

Ben let a long stream of air escape his lips. *Simple. Because I want to get home while Dusty's still there. Because I'd rather see my twenty-three-year-old handyman than spend time with my fiancé. I'm in very serious trouble.*

Dusty inspected the installation of the drywall in the new service porch and laundry room, trying hard not to look toward the front door. *He's having sex with his fiancé. You got a problem with that?*

He swallowed hard. The sad fact was he did. Knowing where Ben was made Dusty want to scream and cry and beat against the walls. *All bad.*

"So how's it look, man?" Artie leaned in through the new doorframe.

"What? Oh, good. Good job."

"Thanks. We gave it a little extra zhuzh just for you." He winked.

Dusty laughed, startled. Not a lot of guys used that word, especially blue-collar guys. Unless, of course, they were gay. He cocked his head at Artie, who was still giving him a cutish leer. Artie was a nice-looking dude in an unexceptional sort of way—medium height, brown hair, lean and wiry. Not six-foot fabulous with hair like a banked fire and emeralds for eyes. *Damn.* Dusty nodded. "Appreciate that."

"So we're all going out for beers after we finish at noon. Want to meet us?"

Dusty gave him a level gaze. "You finish at noon?"

"Half day on Saturday. So, want to come?"

"I don't drink."

"Hell, man, that's no fun." But he laughed good-naturedly. "You an alcoholic or something? That why you don't drive or drink?"

"Oh no, nothing like that."

"Well, if you change your mind, just text me and I'll come get you." He held out a hand. Dusty stared at it, then grinned and handed over his phone. Artie tapped in a message and handed it back. "You could have root beer."

"I'll let you know, okay?" It was nice to be wanted.

"We finished the drywall in the back bedrooms. Tell your boss he should plan to move out of his room for a couple days while we install the floor."

Dusty followed Artie to the end of the hall and peeked into one of the back bedrooms. Man, it was such a nice room. Bright and sunny in the morning, with a big closet and its own bathroom. What would it be like to live in a room as pretty as this? "Finish in this room first, and then we can clean it up so he can move in here while you install his floor."

"Man, Shane sure hired the right guy. You do take good care of your boss." Artie gave him a sideways look.

Dusty jumped a foot when the voice behind him said, "He sure does."

Dusty pressed a hand against his chest, where his heart beat much too hard. "You're good at sneaking up."

"Sorry." Ben smiled, and Dusty's pulse increased even more.

Artie said, "I was just telling Dusty that we need to move into your master next week to do the floor."

"Including the closet?"

"Yes, we want to continue the floor in there, right?"

"Yes. That'll be the hard part, but I'll figure out a way."

"I'll be glad to help." Dusty jotted it in his notebook. When he looked up, Ben smiled at him.

Artie slapped the wall. "Okay, we're done for the day. We'll see you on Monday at 7:00 a.m."

"Do you need me moved out of the bedroom and the closet by then?"

"No, but we'll likely be ready for the floor in there by Tuesday, so you better get started." He grinned. "Considering how many hours you work."

Ben nodded.

Artie looked at Dusty. "Remember. Just call if you want to join us for a beer, okay?" He grinned. "A root beer."

Dusty glanced quickly at Ben, then back at Artie. "Yes. Thanks."

Artie winked, then left the room.

When Dusty looked back up at Ben, there was a crease between his eyebrows. Dusty cleared his throat. "You got here, uh, earlier than I expected. Want to go over my notes?"

Ben seemed to drag his eyes back from where Artie had walked away. "Yeah, that would be great." He walked to his bedroom door and opened it, then pointed toward the chair by the window. "Why don't you sit there and be comfortable, since the rest of the house is such a mess."

"Thank you." Dusty settled into the cushy chair. Nice. The whole room, with its french windows and pretty furniture, was beautiful. "Sitting here reading must be a real pleasure. The light's so nice."

"Yes, it's one of my favorite spots."

"What?" Dusty felt his cheeks heat. "Sorry. I didn't know I said that out loud."

Ben gave him a soft smile. "Not many people notice the light."

"Oh, I do. It's especially nice in the guest room. You'll enjoy it when you stay in there."

Ben sat in the opposite chair, also back to the window, but angled to mostly face where Dusty was sitting.

He was supposed to be giving his report, not admiring the house. He pulled out the notebook. "So you know they replaced the beam with the correct size." He couldn't resist grinning. "The drywall is finished in the laundry room. They did a nice job in there."

"Dusty?"

He looked up and Ben was gazing at him with those deep eyes. "Yes?"

"Have you had breakfast?"

"Oh, uh, no. I came straight here." Actually, he didn't admit it, but he wasn't supposed to go without food for too long. "But I'll get something on the way home."

"You don't work today?"

"Not usually. Sometimes I get extra shifts, but not today."

"Shifts?"

"At the natural foods supermarket. You know, Mom's?"

"Oh right. I love that place. I shop there a lot. So you work there?"

"Yes. Just stocking and food prep, but it's great. I can get juice and good food for a low price."

"So how would you like to join me for brunch?"

Dusty felt his mouth open. He must look like a flycatcher. "Well, that would be nice, but I—I mean, I don't want you to think—"

"What I think is that I never got any food this morning, and I'd love to have your company."

Dusty couldn't control his smile. "Oh man, I'd love to."

CHAPTER SIX

Ben settled in across from Dusty at a table on the covered patio at the small, simple Mediterranean restaurant that served lunch and dinner during the week and added breakfast only on the weekends. But it had organic vegetables and whole-grain breads, which seemed important to Dusty. Funny for a young guy to be so concerned with nutrition. But nice.

The waiter hustled over. "Can I get you something to drink?"

Ben said, "Coffee, please. With cream."

Dusty smiled. "Water's fine."

"Would you like orange juice? They have fresh-squeezed." Ben tried to encourage Dusty. Maybe he thought he shouldn't order anything expensive.

Dusty glanced up from his menu. "No, thanks. Too much sugar."

The waiter raised an eyebrow, probably at the dis to his juice, but he walked away and Dusty kept surveying the menu.

"See anything that you like?"

"Oh yes, thank you." His even teeth flashed at Ben. What a puzzle he was.

"You know a lot about nutrition. Hell, most guys your age live on pizza, beer, and soda."

Dusty shrugged. "I have some health issues, so I had to learn early." He smiled and looked around the restaurant. "I never knew about this place. It's great."

The waiter came back over. Ben tried not to look as interested as he was in what Dusty would order.

"Can I have scrambled eggs with spinach and extra feta cheese with salad on the side, please? I'd like oil and vinegar, and please bring them to the table so I can add them myself."

Ben felt a little decadent ordering his eggs on toast with pesto and avocado, but he did it.

Dusty's face lit up. "Oh, could I have some avocado too?"

When the waiter typed it all into his iPad and left, Ben asked, "You're not trying to lose weight, are you?"

"Heck, no." He glanced at his water glass, then said, "Tell me how you got to work for the foundation."

That warmed Ben's chest. He loved talking about the foundation. "I have a degree in business, and I worked for my dad growing up. But I guess I saw a lot of people who didn't have a chance to prosper because of prejudice, infirmity, lack of role models and opportunity." He shrugged.

Dusty nodded. "That's sure true. I never had a dad like yours. If my mom hadn't been such a hard worker, I might never have learned what you can do if you put your mind to it."

Ben smiled. That seemed like one piece of the Dusty puzzle. No task seemed too small for him to want to do well. Ben said, "I just couldn't bring myself to ignore that there were people not as lucky as me, so after college I joined the Peace Corps, and then when I got back, I went to work for a nonprofit." He sighed and ran his hand through his hair. "But the nonprofits don't have a business ethic a lot of the time. They have no sense of profit and loss or the value of things, and they're riddled with politics. So I got disgusted with the nonprofit world. That's when I heard about ClearWater and the foundation. Here was a chance to run a charitable organization based on sound business principals, and I jumped at it." He glanced at Dusty, who leaned on his hand and smiled as he stared at Ben. "Sorry. I didn't mean to conduct a monologue."

"Man, I love that."

"What?"

"Making a nonprofit run efficiently." Dusty shook his head. "It's like the insurance system. What a crock. All the money gets disbursed at the top, and nothing reaches the people who're supposed to receive it. The same thing happens in charities sometimes." He frowned.

"Yes, it does." Something in Ben's chest wanted to burst out at the thrill of talking to someone about what he loved and getting an equally passionate response.

Dusty stared into space. "Politicians say people who need help want a handout, but it always looks like the executives in these so-called nonprofits are the ones with their hands out." His eyes focused on Ben. "I love that you're running the ClearWater Foundation differently."

"Yes, we try. There's still a lot of politics as well as graft and corruption, both outside the US and even inside. It can be tough to get the money where it belongs if you don't want to play the games."

"I'll bet."

Ben cocked his head. "Sounds like you speak from experience."

"Yeah, I guess." The fire in his eyes banked, and he glanced at the table.

The food arrived at that moment, and Ben watched Dusty slather his salad with enough olive oil to grease a male stripper, but he ate it heartily.

"What do you want to do with your programming skills?"

Dusty shrugged. "I'm not sure." Then he grinned. "Working in a company like your foundation would sure be great. If I can ever finish my degree, I'll send you a résumé."

"I'll look forward to it." Their eyes met, and the truth of that statement burned into Ben's heart. "When will you be finished with school?"

Dusty smiled, but it didn't quite reach his eyes. "Not sure. So tell me how you found your great house."

Ben knew a deflection when he heard it, but since his house was another of his favorite topics, he succumbed and told Dusty all about finding this run-down cottage and living in it while he dreamed of what it could be.

After a few minutes, when the food ran out completely and Ben couldn't manage one more cup of coffee, he finally produced his credit card and plopped it on the check. "I really appreciate you listening to me go on about all this stuff." He smiled.

"Stuff?"

"My house and my job. You know, me, me, me. Sorry." He raised his shoulders and dropped them to release the tension. "I guess most of the people I know don't really like it or care about it that much." Funny how oddly true that was. His folks loved him, but they could never quite figure out why he didn't use his business skills to make more money. Alan couldn't understand why he worked at all when he could just be supported in style, and he thought Ben's house was a waste of real estate.

"But you have such a wonderful life." Dusty smiled sweetly.

Ben inhaled. *Sweet Jesus, it's true.* He looked away because his eyes burned.

A warm hand gripped his forearm, and Ben glanced at Dusty, who stared at him with a quizzical if compassionate look. "Don't you?"

"Yes, yes, I do. I have a great life. I guess like a lot of people, I get so focused on the details, I miss the big picture."

"Any time you want to know how beautiful your life is, you can ask me, okay?" Dusty laughed, and Ben joined in.

"Do you have to go home?"

"No." Dusty's cheeks got a touch of pink.

"Do you like movies?"

"Oh my God, yes." He whispered like he was in church.

"How about a Saturday afternoon movie?"

"Don't you have to work?"

Ben gazed at Dusty. Yes, he had a half day of work planned. Hell, he'd told Alan it was essential. Work was better than anything. "No, I don't."

Almost anything.

Two hours later, Ben stared at the screen and tried to make sense of the story. It was a caper movie with some laugh-out-loud funny scenes and a few serious-as-fuck incidences of violence. But the feature presentation for Ben was the occasional brush of Dusty's arm against his, the sound of his laughter, bright and joyous, and his cute cringing from the scary parts.

No popcorn. No soda. But Dusty still seemed to be having a good time, and maybe he didn't get to do that real often. Hell, he'd never been to Disneyland. An image of Dusty screaming on Space Mountain filled Ben's brain screen.

When the movie ended, they walked around the shopping complex in which the theater was located. Again, Dusty refused frozen yogurt, but in a pet store, Dusty should have been put on video and posted on Instagram under #cutenessoverload. He pressed his nose against the glass, and when the attendant asked if he wanted to go in, he practically ran, petting cats until their fur should have fallen off.

Finally he walked out of the adoption center looking a little misty-eyed. "I guess I better get home."

"You sure? I'll bet we can find another movie."

For a second he brightened, and then his face fell. "No. I should go."

As they crossed the parking lot to the car, Ben said, "Do you have a pet at home?"

Dusty shook his head. "My mom's allergic."

"Oh, I'm sorry."

"Yeah."

This time Ben did open the door for Dusty, since he happened to be on that side of the car. As they rode toward Anaheim, Dusty seemed thoughtful. Maybe a little sad.

"If you could have a pet, would you want a cat or a dog? Or maybe a gerbil?"

That made Dusty giggle. "Maybe a giraffe?"

"We'll get it at GiraffeCo."

"Or GiraffeSmart."

The mood lightened.

Dusty looked out the window beside him, but he said, "I wouldn't care. Cat, dog, whatever wanted me."

Oh crap. Ben's eyes heated. "Uh, so what did you think of the movie?"

"Oh, it was great. Didn't you love the way they used the music? It was so original."

"Yes, I agree." Truth? He'd barely noticed, but now that

he thought of it, the music had been used well. "Want some Chopin?"

"Yes, please." Dusty smiled.

A piano concerto accompanied them the rest of the way up the freeway. Dusty closed his eyes and seemed to float with the melodic strains. As they turned off Katella to approach Dusty's house, Ben said, "So, how come you haven't got a boyfriend at school?" *Shit! Where did that come from?*

Dusty's lashes fluttered and his eyes opened. He shrugged.

Ben swallowed. "Haven't met anyone you like?"

Dusty's head turned slowly toward the window, and he spoke so softly Ben could barely hear him. "I haven't met anyone I like—*at school.*"

As they drove into the cul-de-sac, Dusty looked to the left, and his eyes widened. Ben followed his line of sight. A woman stood on the porch of the ragged house. As Ben's car slowed, she stepped down, frowning, and walked across the lawn, radiating disapproval.

A soft sigh came from Dusty.

Well, damn. Dusty was twenty-three. Couldn't he go to the movies?

As soon as Ben parked at the curb, Dusty opened the passenger door and jumped out. "I'm sorry, Mom. Ben asked me to breakfast and a movie, and I didn't realize how late it was. I should have called you."

She crossed her arms. "Ben?"

Ben walked across the lawn. "Mrs. Kincaid, I'm Ben Shane. Dusty and I work at the same company, and he's also doing some construction supervision for me." He extended his hand.

She was a pretty woman with fair hair like Dusty's, though she seemed to carry too little weight and too much worry. She stared at his hand like it was a sure carrier of some dreaded virus, managed to disentangle her own hand from her arms, and gave Ben's a quick shake. "Mr. Shane, I appreciate your interest in Dusty, but he works really hard, and this is his one day to rest. He needs sleep. Not to be running around getting overheated and overtired. So thanks again, but he doesn't need to do this anymore."

"Mom." Dusty frowned, and she put a hand on his arm.

"You know I'm right."

Dusty looked up, his big eyes pools of misery. "I really had fun, Ben. Thank you so much. Do you need me Monday morning to check on the contractors?" He frowned, pulled out his notebook, and looked in it. "You need help moving out of your bedroom and closet tomorrow, right?"

Ben glanced at Mrs. Kincaid. "Uh, no. I'm fine. I can move into the other room. No problem."

"But the room needs cleaning. I want to help."

His mother narrowed her eyes. "Dustin, Mr. Shane can afford to hire people to clean his house. He doesn't need you, and you don't need another job. You have plenty to do." She shared her glare with Ben. "Say goodbye and come inside and rest." She turned and walked in the house.

Dusty's eyes got shiny, and he blinked rapidly. "I'm sorry. So sorry. Thank you so much for giving me the chance. I really loved working for you, and I liked the movie so much. Thank you."

"Dusty—"

"I better go." He glanced up, took a step forward in a kind of hop, and planted a warm kiss on Ben's cheek, then rushed into his house and closed the door.

Ben stared after him, his cheek throbbing. Sadly, it was throbbing for more.

Ben turned on his heel, marched to the car, climbed in,

and drove away, gritting his teeth the whole time. *Why can that woman control Dusty? He has a bunch of jobs. He could support himself. If he feels sorry for his mom, he still doesn't need to let her push him around. He should—*

He slapped a hand against the steering wheel.

What the hell? Do I have to take care of everyone? What am I doing to Dusty and to me? He's not my boyfriend. He's not even really my friend. I barely know him and have no say in how he lives his life.

Ben sucked in a breath.

He liked Dusty, but that was the natural reaction of a man to a little hero worship. He'd gotten worn down by people wanting him to be some other way, and it was refreshing to be appreciated for himself. Dusty had nothing to lose by admiring Ben. Well, except his mother's approval. But the kid didn't have a real life yet. Ben did. He had responsibilities that he'd chosen and needed to fulfill. It was time to take off his superhero tights and get back to real life. Time to forget some silly fairy tale.

CHAPTER SEVEN

Half an hour later, he drove into the parking lot at Clear-Water. Jesus, what had he been thinking, trotting off to some dumb movie? Still, he'd worked it out in his mind. He liked Dusty. Everyone liked him. Ben had an inclination to want to help people, and—kidding himself aside—Dusty was flat-out gorgeous. Sexy. Attractive.

He parked and climbed out of the car. *But so is Alan, and I'm committed to him. I'm not a cheater. Besides, having a hookup with Dusty, even if I wasn't engaged, wouldn't be fair to him. He's not some one-night stand. Obviously he has problems, and he needs to work them out. It has nothing to do with me.*

He squared his shoulders and walked a little faster into the empty lobby, onto the elevator, and out across the floor toward his office. Voices came from Craig's office, and Ben made a detour to say hi.

When he glanced in, he found Craig sitting at his desk being kissed by the most adorable young guy. Blond, shaggy-haired, small, and slim, kind of like Dusty. The guy wore tight jeans with a white shirt tucked into them but open to the waist. Underneath was the infamous T-shirt saying *I Would Bottom You So Hard.*

After an unfortunate flash of pure envy, Ben cleared his throat loudly. "Uh, I sure hope this is Jesse." He laughed.

Both guys looked up and grinned. The kisser walked around the desk with his hand extended. "You must be Ben. I've heard so much about you from Craig."

"And you're Jesse." He shook the smaller hand. "But how did you know I'm Ben?"

"Auburn hair, gorgeous as a fashion model, works on weekends just like Craig—who else?"

Craig said, "Got a minute to sit? You're later than usual for a Saturday."

Ben crossed and sat in one of Craig's guest chairs, and Jesse took the other. "I know. I, uh, had some things to do earlier."

Craig grinned. "Good. I hope it was fun."

So fun. Yes. Weirdly the most fun he'd had in ages. Ben looked at Jesse. "So Craig tells me you changed his life." He pointed. "With that T-shirt."

"Yep. I'd been drooling over him from afar for weeks, and then my shirt inspired him to ask me to, uh, well, tutor him."

Ben looked at the T-shirt again and snorted. "What exactly were you tutoring him in?"

"Exactly what you think!" Jesse laughed.

Craig blushed. "Actually, it was a general course in how to be more confident and authoritative. I'd never have gotten this job without him."

"He'd have gotten it, but it might have taken longer." Jesse reached for Craig's hand on the desktop and squeezed it.

Ben swallowed the lump in his throat. "It seems to have worked, Jesse."

Jesse clapped his hands together and flashed his adorable,

slightly crooked teeth. "So when are we all going to get together?"

"We?" Ben breathed. "Oh, me and my fiancé?"

"Unless you plan to bring Dusty?" Craig laughed.

Ben's eyes flashed to Craig. *Breathe. He's kidding.* Ben laughed too, although picturing Alan and Jesse at the same table seemed a touch unlikely. "That would be great. I'll have to check Alan's schedule. Why don't you suggest a time?" If Alan was even speaking to him. He wiped a hand over his face.

"Ben, is everything okay?"

Ben looked up. "Oh sure, I—" Suddenly, he didn't want to pretend anymore. He flopped against the chair back and sighed. "Not exactly."

Jesse leaned back in his chair too, as if he was ready to hear. Like he was making a space in his mind—his heart, maybe—for Ben to fill. It reminded him of Dusty listening to Ben talk about his job and his house.

"I'm having trouble settling down—" No, wrong beginning. "I might have made a mistake in getting engaged to Alan." *Whoa. I said it out loud.*

Jesse said, "In what way?"

"He wants somebody who's not me." Also surprising words.

"But he picked you, right?" Craig rotated a glass globe he kept on his desk.

"Yes. Yes, he did. Kind of chased me, in fact. You know how oblivious I can be when I'm working. But he kept calling and saying he wanted to be with me."

"And now?" That was Jesse.

"Every time we're together, I sense that he wants me to be a different guy. I jokingly say he's looking for a trophy wife. I guess I'm scared it's not a joke."

Jesse nodded. "Every person needs a wife. The problem is, no one wants to be one."

"Seriously? No one wants a super-rich guy who'll support them?" Ben cocked his head.

"Oh hell, yes, but that's not what I mean. Having someone support you might be great, but who wants their whole existence to be only about aggrandizing someone else? No personal creativity. Nothing of your own that makes a difference. That's the way men made up the wife résumé. Have my kids, clean my house, cook my meals, and make me look good. I'll support you, but you'll get no power in return. None. Zero. Zip. Everything I married you for—your strength, capability, intelligence, and accomplishment—must be subsumed to serving me." He made a rude noise. "That hidden agenda is buried in the consciousness of almost every guy when he gets married. He may not even know it, but it's cultural memory, baby. Not many women abide by it, and that's where the conflict comes in. The guy's shocked. Wait, didn't you agree to be my wife?" He laughed. "Isn't it weird that even gay guys get it?" He bounded up and did a series of sweeping bows. "You be the wife. No, you be the wife. No, you be the wife." He plopped back down. "The only thing that works, gay or straight, is to take turns being the wife. But it's hard to do. Expectations are killer. In our society, money's power. That's why guys want to support their wives and then complain about it. I gather he's got the money."

Ben nodded.

Craig said, "I should have warned you. Jesse's a teacher."

"What can I do?" Ben practically wailed.

"What you're doing. Show him you plan to live a life that's real for you, and that you respect his identity and choices as well. If he wants to live that life with you, where both partners support the other and the one with more money doesn't have the most power, then you're golden." Jesse grinned.

They all stared at their hands quietly.

Finally Ben shrugged. "All your good advice may be moot. I walked out on him this morning and haven't seen or heard from him since. It might be he's with his parents, but he was pretty pissed."

"It sounds like you need a serious sit-down with your fiancé. It could give you both a chance to lay out your expectations." Jesse smiled sympathetically.

Craig grinned. "Or it could be time for a new boyfriend?"

"What?"

"You sure looked interested in Dusty."

"Who's Dusty?" Jesse looked back and forth between them.

"A really cute guy who does all kinds of jobs around here part-time. You should get to know him, Ben."

Ben stared at his jeans. "I, uh, did."

"What?" His smile widened. "When? How?"

"I needed somebody to help with organizing and overseeing the contractors at my house, since I'm here so much. I saw Dusty managing a kid on some shelf-building and hired him."

"That's great. Is he as nice as he seems?"

"Yes." He wanted to say "nicer," but he didn't. "He lives at home, and his mother was all over him about taking another job. I hope I don't lose him."

"You'd love him, Jesse." Craig looked back at Ben. "You see what I mean about Dusty reminding me of Jesse?"

Ben nodded. "Yeah, I do. But Dusty's odd."

"Thanks a lot, you guys." Jesse smirked. "Though I guess odd is better than weird."

"No." Ben gave Jesse a mock punch on his arm. "Dusty's

twenty-three, but he doesn't drive. I mean, doesn't even have a license. He lives at home, and his mom has a lot of control over him. He doesn't drink, eat sugar, or much of anything that's bad for him." He shrugged. "Like I said, odd."

"You really did get to know him." Craig glanced at Jesse with a little smile.

"Yeah." Ben stood slowly. "But I'm too old for him anyway, even if I wasn't engaged."

"You're six years older. How's that too old?"

Ben released a long exhale. "More about where we are in our lives, I guess." He forced a smile. "Thanks for listening, you guys. I better get to work if I ever want to get out of here." Ben walked to the door of Craig's office.

"Ben."

He looked back at Jesse.

"Don't marry somebody because everyone expects you to."

Whoa! Close to home. "Good advice. Thank you." He walked to his office, trying not to let his shoulders slump. He sat in his chair, turned on his computer automatically, and stared at it, but the conversation wouldn't go away.

His phone buzzed, and he looked down. Text.

Don't want to bother you on the weekend, but you're invited to dinner. My place. With my boys. Tuesday night. Bring Alan. LOL. 7:00 p.m. Here's address.

Surprisingly, the address was in Laguna, not Newport.

Anastasia Merced.

Holy crap. He jumped out of his chair and ran down the hall to Crag's office. They were kissing again, and he stopped and laughed.

Craig pulled away from Jesse, blushing. "Sorry."

"Never be sorry." His grin was real this time. "Guess what?"

"What?"

"I've been invited to have dinner on Tuesday with"—he swept a hand in an arc—"Anastasia Merced and her sons."

"Holy crap." Craig looked wide-eyed, and Jesse looked between them like he was viewing a tennis match.

"Who's that?"

Craig said, "One of the richest women in the world, head of one of the richest families in the world."

"Wow."

Ben nodded. "I need the help of your department to do a whiz-bang presentation for her and her sons."

"You got it. When?"

"I'll do some research tomorrow on the best charities to match with the Merceds. Then your people can start the presentation on Monday."

"How do you know this woman?" Jesse looked amazed.

Ben grimaced. "I met her at my engagement party at the Ashlands'."

Jesse widened his eyes. "Oh dear."

"Yeah. She said I should bring Alan to the dinner."

They all stared at each other and sighed. Ben sighed the loudest as he walked back to his office.

Two hours later, he gave it up for the day. He felt like he'd been run over by a damned truck. TMD. Too much drama.

He gathered his stuff. Craig and Jesse had left. Man, he really liked those guys, and how amazing was it to have someone to talk to? And how sad to not have anyone else in his life to whom he could talk—except Dusty. *Don't even think about that.*

He leaned against the wall of the elevator and closed his eyes for a minute. From the depth of his soul, he wanted Anastasia Merced's money for his foundation. Hell, with just a piece of that fortune, they could feed every hungry child in

America. Treat every AIDS patient in Africa. *That* he wanted. Everything else in his life felt like chaotic crap.

The bell dinged, and he stepped off into the softly lighted lobby with only the guard at the desk. "Good night, Carlos."

"Night, Mr. Shane."

Ben walked into the parking lot, breathing in the cool night air. Visitors were never prepared for the twenty and thirty degree differences in temperature between day and night in southern California. There wasn't enough humidity to hold much heat.

He pulled his car key from his pocket and stopped. Ahead, his Lexus sat alone in the parking lot—if you didn't count the Ferrari parked next to it.

How do I feel about this? Good. Get it resolved.

As he walked forward, Alan stood on the driver's side of his car and looked over the hood at Ben. "Hi."

"Hi."

"You're late."

"Yes."

"I guess I've been saying this a lot, Ben, but I'm sorry. I was out of line. I'm having trouble reconciling how we live together, but I want to do it. I want to figure it out and make it work."

Ben leaned on the opposite side of Alan's car. He sucked a breath. "Why?"

"What?" Alan frowned.

"I'm not being snarky. I'm serious. Why do you want to make it work with me when it's so much trouble? There are hundreds, thousands of guys who'd be happy to compromise down to the ground to have a gorgeous, intelligent, rich guy support them. Why me when I'm so much work?"

"I care about you."

The absence of the word *love* didn't escape Ben, but in all fairness, he wasn't sure he could say it either. "I get that. Thank you."

Alan shrugged. "Maybe it's because you don't compromise. You are who you are, and I admire that."

"I'm not sure how much you'll admire it when I'm late for some family dinner for the tenth time." Ben smiled.

"I'm not either, but I'll expect you to do some compromising too."

The passion to scream *What do you think I've been doing for the last year?* almost overwhelmed him, but he kept his lips pressed together. He cleared his throat. "I'm having dinner at Anastasia Merced's on Tuesday night. Do you want to come?"

A ghost of a smile whispered across Alan's lips. Sure, he knew when he'd won. "That's wonderful for you. Of course, I'd love to go. Remy Merced and I were in school together, and John Jack is a fan of my dad's."

Of course they are. "I'm looking forward to meeting them."

"So, do you want to come to my place?"

"No. I have to move out of my bedroom and closet tomorrow so they can put in the floors next week."

Alan sighed but said, "So I should pick you up on Tuesday?"

"Yes. We have to be there at 7:00 p.m., but since they're in Laguna, it shouldn't take long."

Alan waved a hand. "There's always some kind of red tape at their gate, so I'll pick you up at 6:30."

"Okay."

Ben turned and got in his car. Before he closed the door, Alan said, "I really am sorry about pushing you."

Ben smiled and nodded. That's all he could manage before he closed the door and drove away.

CHAPTER EIGHT

SHIT. BEN pushed the clothes aside and squeezed another
sports coat into the guest room closet. He'd forgotten how
little storage there was in the house since he'd turned the
fourth bedroom into a walk-in.

He stopped, stood straight, and stretched his back. He'd
cleaned the closet floor with a sponge, which was more
bending over than he was used to. *Where the hell am I going to
put the rest of the clothes?* He'd admit to having kind of a luxurious wardrobe for a guy. His mom said his love of clothes was
her first clue he was gay. Now he got to pay the price.

He turned and gazed around the guest room. If he could get
this room cleaned up and the bed made, maybe he could push one
of his chairs from his bedroom in here, or maybe two, and stack
clothes on them. First he had to get the bed out of the way without
scratching the brand-new wooden floors so he could mop them.

He peered under and nodded approvingly at the cushion
pads that had been applied to the legs of the bed. Man, that
piece of thoughtfulness reeked of Dusty.

He sighed. *Don't go there.* He applied his shoulder to the

bed, sliding it against the wall. *Cleaning supplies. Where the hell are they?* He walked out to the kitchen and peered into the laundry room. Nothing in there, of course, since the room had been stripped and redone. *Okay, where?* He looked under the sink and found some biodegradable cleaning stuff, but no bucket. *And the mop? Shoot.*

He ran a hand through his hair and poured a cup of coffee. Another cup. He needed lots of caffeine to deal with this day. No wonder Alan hated being in Ben's house.

A soft tapping made him turn. *Was that the door?* Ben took another sip as he flip-flopped toward the door, his baggy, holey jeans swishing around his legs. As he approached, the door opened. "Oh."

"Oh." Dusty stood in the doorway, poised like an undecided cat.

"Sorry. You startled me." At least, his heart was beating like a hammer. How could he forget in a day how wonderful it was to look at that beautiful face?

"Sorry. I thought you weren't home, and I was going to come in and get started."

"Started?"

"On cleaning out your bedroom."

"But your mom—"

"I told my mom I was working for you and I keep my commitments."

Ben shook his head. "You don't have to do that, Dusty. She said you needed to rest, and I'm guessing she knows what she's talking about."

"No. I'm here to help." He glanced at Ben. "Looks like you started."

"Did you eat?"

"Yes."

"Do you know where the mop and bucket are? Please?" Ben clasped his hands together and laughed.

Dusty grinned. "Why, yes, as a matter of fact I do."

"My hero."

Dusty took off at speed toward the kitchen with Ben following him. Dusty walked out the back door and a peek out the window showed him going in the side door of the detached garage. He emerged a minute later with a bucket and not one, but two mops. Now why hadn't that occurred to Ben?

Ben met him on the back steps, grabbed one of the mops and the bucket, and went to fill it in the kitchen, his heart lighter than it had been in twenty-four hours. He caught himself smiling. If he were a good man, he'd be concerned about Dusty getting enough rest, but all Ben felt was happy.

He powered into the guest room, stuck the mop in the warm, slightly bubbly water, and started cleaning the floor.

"Uh, Ben?"

"Yes?" The smile still clung to his lips.

"We should dust and clean all the high areas first. The windowsills, tops of the dresser and nightstands. Otherwise the dirt will just fall on the clean floor."

Ben leaned on his mop handle, swamped with a mini-wave of upper-middle-class white guy privilege. He hadn't cleaned a damned thing since he was seven—until today. "Thank you. I cleaned the floor of the closet but not the shelves."

"I mean, you can do it however—"

He held up a hand. "No, I'm serious. Thank you for telling me how to do it correctly. I'll get some sponges and towels." Laughing at himself, he hurried back to the kitchen.

When he returned, Dusty was looking at the clothes he'd crammed in the closet. "We need to cover these with towels before I dust the shelves." He'd found a stepladder and had it poised in front of the closet.

"Okay." Off again he went to the linen cabinet and grabbed some old towels from the back.

Dusty was already on the stepladder when Ben handed him the towels. He carefully laid them over Ben's clothes like he was protecting the Mona Lisa, and then began to scrub at the top shelf.

For a second Ben let himself admire those lean legs in tight, worn denim, and then he plunged into work, washing down all the high surfaces in the room. When he finished his side of the space, he re-wet the mop, wrung it to bare dampness, and started the floors. The new wooden surface shone as he wiped the damp sponge over it.

Dusty mopped from the opposite corner of the room. "We'll probably have to go back over this since there's so much dust. It's likely to streak."

"Anything you say, boss." Ben grinned, and Dusty flashed his dimples back. Ben put some Chopin on his phone, and the beautiful music filled the room.

When they both arrived at the door to the hall at the same time, Ben stopped and looked around. "You're right. The floor will need another pass. I was thinking I could move the chairs from my bedroom in here and pile the rest of my clothes on them."

"More?" Dusty's wide eyes showed he wasn't kidding.

"Yeah, sorry. I'm a real clotheshorse."

"What a funny expression." Dusty smiled.

"Want some tea?" He remembered Dusty's aversion to coffee.

"No, thanks. I don't do well with caffeine in anything."

"I may have some herb tea, and I've got lots of water."

"Okay, thanks."

They walked toward the kitchen. Ben said, "That horse expression comes from the name for a clothes-drying rack back in the day. They called it a clotheshorse." He glanced at Dusty. "I know because I looked it up after being called one a few times."

In the kitchen, he searched for herb tea. The box he found in the back of his pantry didn't look promising. "I think they delivered this one on the Mayflower."

Dusty snorted. "Water's fine." He got out two glasses and filled one with ice that he handed to Ben, and then got his own water from the sink purifier. Dusty leaned against the counter and sipped, looking impossibly like some James Dean lookalike with fairer hair—the same combination of innocence and experience, self-protection and vulnerability. "So you like clothes?"

"Yeah."

"Why, do you think?"

Ben shrugged. "I didn't come out until high school. I guess clothes were a way to express myself before I actually became myself."

"Why did you come out? High school's hard."

That sounded like the voice of experience. "There was a guy I really liked, and everyone knew he was gay. There was no way to be his boyfriend in secret, so I had to choose."

"And you chose love." Dusty smiled softly, almost to himself.

"I guess so, to the extent that a fifteen-year-old's passion is love."

"Romeo and Juliet." Dusty glanced up. "What happened? When you came out, I mean?"

"Some friends dropped me. Some didn't. I got quietly pushed off the baseball team, even though I was a really good player." He felt his lips turn up. "But I didn't care. My folks had already guessed, so little drama there, and the boy I liked, liked me back. Oh yeah. He had a fair amount of experience for a sixteen-year-old, and he spent the summer teaching me what all my adolescent hormones were for. I didn't mind at all." He looked up at Dusty, who gazed at him with glassy eyes. He slowly wet his lips. Ben cleared his throat. "Uh, what about you? When did you come out?"

"Oh." He raised his shoulders and dropped them. "Never, I guess. I always knew, so I just told people and that was all."

Ben mimicked Dusty's words from earlier. "Did you have a really tough time in high school?"

A look of pain crossed his face. "Not because I was gay, really." He sucked a breath. "Back to work?" He pushed away from the counter.

"All right."

In the bedroom, Dusty grabbed the bucket and carried it out, returning a couple of minutes later with clean water smelling like vinegar.

Ben wrinkled his nose. "You made a salad?"

"White vinegar's great for cleaning wood floors. I found a bottle in your pantry and added a little to the water. You shouldn't use much regular chemical stuff on these nice floors."

"Anything you say." He flashed his teeth again at Dusty, turned the music back on, and they went to work.

A few strokes in, Dusty glanced over at Ben and sped up his mopping. Ben got faster to match Dusty, and then added a little more speed.

Dusty started mopping like crazy, and Ben copied him, stroke for stroke. Dusty giggled as he wrung out the mop with super speed and went back to his mad moparama.

Ben gritted his teeth, slopped some water on the floor, and spread it around at double time.

Dusty yelled, "No fair. You can't splash water on this floor!"

"Okay, okay." Ben grabbed a cloth and dried the floor as Dusty got ahead of him in the race to the door. Ben snatched his mop, wrung it out, and went into overdrive, swiping like a Mr. Clean fanatic.

Dusty laughed, and Ben laughed with him as they backed toward the wall, angling toward the door.

Dusty yelled, "I'm winning."

"Don't even dream it!"

Adrenaline rushed through Ben as he cleaned his last few feet of hardwood. His butt hit something hard and soft at the same time that turned out to be Dusty's perfect ass. Dusty yelped and spun, thrusting forward his mop like a rapier. Ben met him and they began to fence with crossed mops, howling like loons.

Aluminum handles clanked and beads of water sprayed all over them as they danced around the room.

"Oh!" Suddenly, Dusty's foot hit a damp patch, his arms flew up as his feet slid out from under him, and he pinwheeled backward, arms and mop flailing.

Ben dodged the swinging cleaning device and grabbed Dusty just before his head hit the wall. Dusty fell forward and landed against Ben's chest, throwing him off balance despite the size difference, and the two of them careened backward like the tree that fell in the forest when no one was listening. Ben reached out an arm behind him and managed to hurl his body, still holding Dusty, toward the bed that had been pushed against the wall.

His butt hit the mattress, legs still flailing, but he managed to keep Dusty from landing on the floor by hauling him against his body.

"Whoa! Holy crap, that was close."

When Ben realized they were both okay, he started to laugh—until his current position soaked in, and in, and in.

Dusty lay almost fully on top of him, legs between Ben's, hanging over the edge of the bed, which brought their groins into very tight proximity. Clearly, before Ben's big brain had even noticed, his little brain pronounced its pleasure at the pressure. And more to the point, Dusty's erection demonstrated it was way more than happy to see him too.

Oh hell, that feels so good.

Little brain became huge brain became controlling brain, and Ben pressed his mouth to those lush, full, slightly pouty lips that had been driving him to madness for weeks.

Oh sweet heaven. Dusty's mouth opened, not even hesitantly but with the same enthusiasm his penis was demonstrating, and his arms wrapped around Ben, a funny little whimpering noise coming from somewhere inside the column of his perfect throat.

Ben let his tongue explore. Dusty smelled like sweat and vinegar and some divinely sweet, devilishly spicy scent between flowers and cinnamon and cloves that must come from an herbal store. His taste? Amazing. How could a guy who never ate sugar taste so much like cookies? Ben loved cookies. Wanted to eat cookies. Cookie monster. He giggled somewhere in his gut, but never pulled away—

—until Dusty's legs wrapped around Ben's hips and that contact went from hot to immediate, compelling, undeniable, brain-sucking, nervous-system-swamping lust. *Shit!* Lust for a guy who—*no!*

Ben rolled to the side, pushing Dusty under him, and leaped from the bed backward, almost replicating the move he'd saved Dusty from before, until he staggered into the opposite wall. "Oh God, I'm sorry. I'm so sorry."

Dusty propped on his elbows, then sat up slowly, staring at Ben as if he'd crammed his pajama pockets with cobras.

Sweet Jesus, what have I done? "I'm so sorry, Dusty. I just lost it. I—you're—I mean, you're very attractive, and I just forgot, and I should know better and be more responsible. And I'm so, so sorry."

Dusty nodded. "Of course. I understand. I'm sorry too." He stood slowly, and Ben could practically watch Dusty's erection folding up in his jeans. "I should have known better. I guess I just wanted to be around—" He never looked at Ben once. His shoulders slumped and his head hanging, he walked out the door of the bedroom.

Before Ben could even get the conviction to push away from the wall, he heard the front door close.

Wait!

He flew out of the room and ran toward the front, tripping himself on his flip-flops more than once. He ripped open the door and raced outside. "Dusty!"

Gone. No Dusty on the sidewalk or anywhere Ben could see. Like aliens had picked him up the second he'd run outside, leaving a message that said *If you don't appreciate him, we'll take him back.*

Gone, like he'd never even been there.

If you didn't count the gaping hole in Ben's heart.

CHAPTER NINE

"Dusty, honey what's wrong?" His mom rushed to him as he practically fell through the door into the living room. No way to hide. He knew his tearstained face said more than he could excuse.

"Nothing, Mom. I just need to lie down."

"Dammit, Dustin. I told you not to go." She took a deep breath. She tried so hard not to blame him for going against her wishes. She tried to treat him like an adult. "So you're just tired? You don't have flashes?"

"Yes, ma'am." He wanted to scream and cry and rail against the shimmering halos that circled his field of vision and made it hard to walk. "I'm going to take a nap, okay? Then I'd love something to eat. Something good." He flashed her the warmest, happiest, most believable smile he could muster.

She fell for it. "Okay, honey. How about some nice salmon and mashed potatoes with lots of butter?"

"That sounds perfect." He tried to walk a straight line to his room. When he got inside, he carefully closed the door, then struggled to the bed and fell on it. Clutching his belly—

or maybe his heart—he curled in a ball. Salmon? He knew how much she had to pay for it to give him the high-fat fish, but God, he didn't care if he never ate again.

Breathe. Deeply. Breathe.

The air filled his belly, then his chest, and then expanded all the way behind his collarbone. *Peace. Joy. Peace. Joy. He didn't want me. He realized what a mistake he made and ran. Peace. Please, peace.*

He breathed and focused on the breath. Again and again. *Stop. Why on earth would he want me? All shall be well. It's as it should be. All shall be well.*

The welcome gray fog of sleep crept across his brain.

"BEN, ARE you okay?"

Ben looked up from the PowerPoint slides flashing on his laptop screen at Craig, who sat beside him at his conference table. "Yeah. I'm fine."

Craig smiled. "You don't seem quite as elated—or as nervous—as I thought you'd be at the impending meeting with the Merceds."

"Hey, with a great presentation like this, why be nervous?" That was true. Craig's people had done an amazing job of gathering the statistics he needed and turning them into a moving and compelling story he looked forward to sharing with Anastasia and her sons. But of course, that wasn't all that was true for Ben. He let his phony smile drop. "I'm just having, I don't know, mixed emotions. I feel like I have a host of hidden agendas. That're so secret they're even hidden from me." He gave a tight half grin.

"Hell, that's how most of us are when it comes to ourselves. So it's your fiancé you have the mixed feelings about?"

"Yeah. That and other things. But I almost cheated on Alan the other day, and I'm not a fucking cheater, so I know I need to deal with my issues before they push me into being someone I don't want to be."

"Is it all about sex?"

"I don't think so, but that has something to do with it." He sat back. *Get over yourself.* "I'm going with him to the Merceds' tonight, so maybe I'll get to resolve some of my uncertainties."

Craig raised his eyebrows. "Right. He's the author of the feast, right? You met the Merceds through your fiancé's family."

"Yes. Did I mention he's rich?" He made a side smirk.

"But the fact is, you don't much care about money from what I've seen."

Ben ran his hands over his hair. "The people we try to help would say I don't care about money because I've never had to."

Craig just nodded.

"Let's wrap this up." He let out his breath and tried to relax his stomach. "I've only got three hours 'til show time."

"Sure. So on the next to the last slide, you want—"

"Craig, have you seen Dusty?"

"What? Oh yeah. It's not his regular day, but I think I saw him earlier doing some more work in the library. They must have given him an extra assignment. The kid's got skills." He flipped through the slides.

Ben tried to master his brain. All the previous day, he'd jumped every time someone walked by his office. He'd called and texted Dusty countless times, apologizing for being such an ass, for taking advantage of him, for everything including breathing, but no answer. None. Shit, he'd called HR to be sure Dusty hadn't quit, but they assured him he hadn't.

I have to see him. He rose.

"Oh, are we done?"

"Sorry. I just—sorry." He ran out the door and toward the library.

As he got close to the room—which was really more of a relaxing space full of video games and ebooks that could be borrowed than an actual library—Dusty was walking out the door.

Ben stopped. Dusty looked as bad as it was possible for his angel face to look. Pale, with dark circles under his eyes, and his mouth compressed tightly in a line. "Dusty?"

Dusty looked up. For an instant his face softened; then a deep crease slashed between his light brows, and he shook his head.

"Dusty, please let me explain." Jesus, he wasn't quite sure what he wanted to explain. Could he explain how he wanted Dusty so badly he could barely control his idiot heart? How he really cared about him and wanted only good things for him and knew that he, Ben, wasn't what Dusty really needed? Did he want to try to talk about how he'd gotten himself committed to a relationship for the first time in his life, after avoiding commitment forever, and now he'd feel like a failure if he just tossed it? And even if he did, he had no right to be with Dusty, who was so young and beautiful and perfect and fresh, and Ben already felt like a has-been. How could he say all that? "Dusty, I'm so sorry."

Dusty frowned ferociously. "You shouldn't be sorry. I did it. I knew when I got there, I only came to your house because I wanted to see you so much, and you didn't really need me and I should have stayed away, and then I lured you and tried to get you to like me when that's stupid, and—" Dusty stumbled and Ben took a step forward, but Dusty threw a hand toward him. "I should go. I need to go." He broke into a run, pushing right past Ben and down the hall.

When Ben turned to follow, he almost gasped because a small crowd of people stood there staring, Craig among them. *Damn, did they hear what Dusty said? What do they think?* His eyes met Craig's and he saw nothing but compassion, but over Craig's shoulder, Ben watched Dusty turn toward the lobby. His body rebelled. *I don't give a shit what they think!* "Dusty!"

He took off down the hall, running as fast as his gym-trained body would let him. *I'll never get there in time, but I'll go to his house and wait. I'll try to talk to his mother.*

Ben burst through the lobby door and froze. Dusty stood there, staring into space like a statue, not moving at all.

The receptionist leaned over her desk. "Is he okay? Should I call the nurse?"

"Dusty?" He didn't answer. Ben said, "Yes. Call her quick." He looked back at Dusty's beautiful face, now as white and featureless as marble.

Suddenly Dusty's arm twitched, followed by another; then his body folded toward the floor, shaking and writhing like a leaf in a whirlpool.

Ben dove for him, managing to slide a hand under his head so the back of Ben's hand and not Dusty's skull crashed into the polished granite floor. He barely felt the pain as he fell to his knees beside a convulsing Dusty. "Oh my God. God."

Ben felt someone kneel next to him and looked over at Craig. Craig said, "It's a seizure."

"I know. But what should I do?"

Footsteps came up behind Ben. The company nurse displaced Craig next to Ben. "You already did it. Try to keep him from hitting his head."

Ben whipped his suit coat off one arm and slid that hand under Dusty's head as he took off the other sleeve. Then he rolled the coat into a ball. Dusty's frantic movements were subsiding, and Ben slipped the jacket under his head. A little blood oozed from the corner of Dusty's lips, and Ben had to grit his teeth not to scream. "He's bleeding."

The nurse nodded and pulled a packet of sterile gauze from her pocket. "He's bitten his tongue or the inside of his mouth. That's quite common." She reached toward Dusty, and Ben put a hand on her arm. "Let me. Uh, I'm closer."

Gently he wiped at the edge of Dusty's mouth. Dusty's arm lay in front of him, and Ben spied the bracelet. He nodded. "MedicAlert."

The nurse bent her head and inspected it. "Epilepsy. No medication's listed, but there's a number."

Dusty's eyes fluttered open. For a moment he just stared straight ahead, and then he glanced up. "Oh."

"Hey." Ben smiled. It probably revealed way more than was wise, but no help for it. "You had a seizure, I think."

He nodded. "I-I figured." He puffed his cheeks and exhaled, his eyes closing again.

"Dusty, should we call a doctor? Or do you have some medication you need to take?"

He shook his head but didn't open his eyes. "Need to go home."

"Will your mother be there?"

"Don't remember."

The nurse murmured, "Loss of memory is a symptom." She spoke louder. "Dusty, I'm Charlotte Andrews, the nurse here at ClearWater. I can take you home and wait with you until your mother gets there, okay?"

Ben's whole being rebelled, but he bit the inside of his cheek to keep from blurting out more idiocy.

"C-could Ben take me?" Dusty didn't open his eyes.

Did he just float ten feet off the floor? Ben nodded his head and tried to keep the sap from rising into his grin. "Sure I can."

Dusty sighed and pressed his face into Ben's folded jacket.

Charlotte stood and waggled a finger for him to follow. She walked a few steps away. He rose and followed her. She said softly, "It would be good for you to take him, since he knows you and feels comfortable with you. Stress is a major trigger of seizures in some people with epilepsy."

Well, damn. "He was pretty upset before he had the seizure, partly with me, I think."

"Oh?" She raised an eyebrow. "He may not remember much of what occurred earlier today and possibly even yesterday. But if you're at odds, maybe it's better if I go."

"Oh no, nothing like that. We just had a misunderstanding when Dusty was, uh, doing some work for me." Dusty's upset face from earlier in the hall flashed in Ben's mind. *God, he must not remember.*

"He seems to trust you now. I can try to call his mother. I'm sure they have the phone number on file in the office if the one on his bracelet isn't for his home."

"No, it's okay. His mother's a nurse and I know where he lives, so I'll take him and wait for her if she's not there." He turned. "Craig, would you help me get Dusty into my car."

Craig's brows pulled together briefly. Then he said, "Sure, Ben. Uh, are you going to be back in time to go to your dinner with Anastasia Merced?"

Holy blessed crap. He'd forgotten all about it.

. . .

Dusty breathed deeply, leaning against the cushy leather car seat, trying to clear the fog and exhaustion that always followed a seizure. Deep inside, some piece of his brain screamed *Why?* Why, after a full year of no seizures, did he wind up on the floor at ClearWater? He was so careful.

The reason lay just beyond the black hole of missing memory.

Relax. It comes back. He knew that. After a few hours, or days, the missing pieces would drift in, always shrouded with a little mist.

Right now he wanted to appreciate feeling safe with Ben. If Ben weren't driving, Dusty would have had trouble keeping himself from crawling onto his lap. He frowned. *We don't have that kind of relationship, do we?*

"Dusty?" Ben had such a soothing voice.

"Um-hm?"

"Is it okay to talk to you? Do you feel up to it?"

"Sure." That might be true.

"How long have you had epilepsy?"

He couldn't get his eyes to open, so he stopped fighting. "All my life. It was childhood onset, and sometimes that goes away. I haven't had any seizures or bad episodes in over a year. I thought—I thought as long as I was careful—" His throat closed, and he stopped talking or he'd cry.

"So that's why you're so picky about food and what you drink and everything, right? And why you can't drive?"

Dusty nodded. "I hoped I could drive soon—" The last came out on a hiccup. *I should shut up.*

"What do you think brought it on?" Ben's voice sounded strained. It was tough to be around someone having a bad seizure.

"I don't know exactly. I guess I've been pretty busy and worrying more. All of that's bad, but it shouldn't be enough."

He sighed. "I'll remember later." A wave of pure exhaustion washed over him.

"Uh, I think I might have had something to do with it."

"Why?"

"You've been working for me—"

"Oh, that's okay, Ben. I really enjoy it." That was true, but Ben and his mom were right. He'd probably done too much. Still, he liked doing things for Ben.

Dusty wanted to keep talking to Ben, but the waves sucked him under. As he drifted into sleep, Ben said, "I really like you, and I don't want to be the cause of upsetting you—"

That's nice. He fell asleep.

CHAPTER TEN

THE *DING* of his phone rang through the quiet living room as Ben sat on the edge of the worn couch and listened to low murmurs coming from down the hall. He grabbed his phone. The text from Alan said *Where the hell are you?*

Shit! He glanced at his watch. Six thirty. *Hellfire.* He hit the button for his favorites and dialed.

"Ben, where are you? I'm standing on your fucking porch."

"I'm so sorry. I had an emergency. I'll meet you at Anastasia's as soon as I can."

"Emergency? Did someone miss a shipment of aspirin to a foster home? For God sake, Ben, this is Anastasia Merced. If you behave badly, it reflects on me and my family."

Every cell in his body screamed *Fuck you!* Except his mouth. That he kept closed. Alan had done him a favor by agreeing to go, and Ben was putting Alan in a terrible position. "I'm sorry. It was a critical issue. I'll leave now."

"Leave? Where are you?"

"I'll be there as soon as I can. Probably a few minutes after seven. I really am sorry."

He hung up, stood, and walked to the hall. *Leave a note.* He moved some papers on a small desk to find a blank one, picked up a pencil, and flipped over a page. *What?* It was a printed email to Dusty's mom. The subject said *Selling the House.* Ben glanced up toward the murmuring voices and then down at the email that told Mrs. Kincaid the owners would be selling the house. He breathed out. Presumably the house he was currently standing in. *Well, shit. Exactly what Dusty needs. More stress.*

He rearranged the papers and tiptoed down the hall to Dusty's tiny bedroom, where his mom was giving him some kind of pills and putting him to bed. Ben leaned in the partly opened door. "I'm sorry. I'm late for an appointment. I have to go. Is he okay?"

Her head snapped up, and she flashed a vicious scowl at Ben that pushed him into the hall without a word. A moment later, she walked out and closed the door after her. "Leave, Mr. Shane. This is your fault. I don't know all the details, but I know my son's been upset and overtired since he met you. I can't blame you. I'm sure Dusty never told you about his health. But now you know. Leave him alone. He doesn't need your work or your stress. He was doing well until he met you. Just leave him alone!" The last was almost a shriek.

Ben tried not to run. "You're right. He never told me or anyone at the company, as far as I know. Maybe HR. But I care about him." He swallowed. "A lot of people at Clear-Water do, and we'd never have hurt him if we'd known." *I mean, I'd never hurt him. Ever.*

She nodded. "I know. I'm sorry for being so upset, but honestly, he's done so well, his doctor allowed him to go off his meds. This has set him back." She shook her head. "I don't even know how far. When he comes out of his fog, I know he's going to be so unhappy."

Ben put a hand on her shoulder, and she glanced at it but didn't shake it off. He said, "If I can do anything—really, anything—please just call me. My number's in Dusty's phone. Ben Shane."

He hurried down the hall and to the front door, and then turned. "I really am sorry."

Trying to shrug the weight of guilt and sadness, he walked to the car and climbed in. *Holy fucking hell. I have to get the presentation.*

Forty-five minutes later, still in his rumpled suit with the sweet smell of Dusty on the jacket, and with the presentation prepared by Craig's marketing team under his arm, he drove into the gate at the Merceds'—one hour late. How could a guy with such exciting possibilities ahead of him feel so fucking miserable?

A guy stopped him in front of the house and tapped on his window. "I'll take your car, sir."

"Good, thanks." He slid out, gave the guy the key, and was met at the door by an anxious butler who escorted him through the grand traditional home into a formal living room. Anastasia Merced sat on the couch beside a man Ben recognized from photos as John Jack Merced, the oldest of her sons. Next to him, a beautiful blonde woman with breasts too big for her thin frame gazed somewhat absently into space. According to press, she was John Jack's trophy wife, Trudy.

Alan rose from a side chair where he sat next to the younger son, Remy. "Dear God, where have you been?" He took a step closer to Ben and kissed his cheek, giving him a lowered-brow frown the others couldn't see.

Ben stepped forward to Anastasia, not brushing off Alan, but also not embracing him. "I'm so sorry to be late. A friend had a serious medical emergency, and I had to be sure he was receiving care before I could leave."

She stood and gave Ben a hug, which she didn't have to do. *Nice of her.* She said, "I'm so sorry. Is everything under control?"

"I think so. Thank you. I left him with a nurse who's familiar with his condition."

Anastasia gave his arm a squeeze. "I hope it's okay. I know how frightening health emergencies can be. When John Jack was real little, we hardly had any health insurance, and I was always trying to take care of him without spending any money. My daddy too."

"I gather my friend's situation is similar."

He looked at John Jack, and Anastasia said, "Here I am going on like some giant earth mother. Ben, this here is my oldest, John Jack, who's CEO of our retail group. That's his wife, Trudy, who I've got to tell you right off is smarter than she looks, so don't underestimate her, and back there is my boy, Remy, who helped Merced Enterprises diversify, which has been our salvation in this changing economy."

Ben shook each of their hands. John Jack had a shrewd but kind of dissipated look that jibed with his reputation for hard living acquired from his father, who had died young. Trudy's big blue eyes flashed an intelligent look behind the carefully adopted vacant expression. He'd read she came from poverty, just like Anastasia. There was probably a story there.

Remy bounded up and pumped Ben's hand. "So happy to meet you, Ben. I know Alan would only choose the best of the best, so I'm honored and really anxious to hear what you have to say."

Some tiny glimmer in Alan's eyes said *See what I do for you.* Or maybe that was just Ben's imagination.

Remy said, "What can we get you to drink?"

A patient waiter stood to the side, smiling pleasantly.

Ben sat in the comfortable upholstered chair that had been left open between Alan and Anastasia. "White wine is fine, and I'm sure I've detained dinner, so please don't wait on me anymore."

"Thanks for that, anyway. We're starving," Alan groused.

Anastasia smiled, but it didn't reach her eyes. "Oh, poor darling. But I've got to tell you, sweetheart, I've seen starving, and it didn't look nothin' like you." She glanced up at the butler hovering on the edges of the group. "Tell the cook to serve anytime, Nigel."

Ben couldn't keep a little smile off his lips at the butler's name.

Anastasia, smarter than the average bear, caught it. "I know, isn't that a kick in the balls? I have a real butler, really named Nigel. Me, little ol' Annie Merced. If you put it in a book, baby, people'd laugh."

John Jack snorted and sucked up another mouthful of some highball he was cradling. According to the story, Anastasia had birthed John Jack in her teens, before the family was wealthy and before she'd become Anastasia. Annie had been her name then, married to Billy Ray Merced. Their pure entrepreneurial guts and ruthlessness had produced all the rest.

Trudy glanced at John Jack. She looked... not exactly uneasy. Maybe more like resigned to his liquor consumption. She didn't echo it, but rather twirled a nearly full wineglass in her fingers. She said, "So you work for a charity, Ben?"

"A lot of them, actually. I head a foundation that raises and contributes money to charities, research projects, even governments that are working to make a significant difference in some kind of global problem."

"That's great. I'd love to do something like that."

John Jack looked up and laughed. "Right. You could assure the preservation of cheerleaders all over the world."

Interestingly, Trudy didn't look stricken or even deeply affected by his demeaning remark. She just raised an eyebrow at him and shrugged.

Angels might fear treading on John Jack's remark, but Remy rushed in. "I think Trudy'd be great at pretty much anything she tried."

John Jack glowered over the rim of his nearly empty glass.

After the death of his father, John Jack, now in his forties, headed the retail division, the primary source of the Merceds' staggering wealth, but the drastic downturn in brick-and-mortar retail was taking a toll, even on the mightiest of giants. As a result, Remy's technology and environmental science enterprises were saving the company's ass. Rumor said there was rivalry between the brothers, one a child of poverty and the other, seven years younger, the baby of the Merceds' boom time. The tension vibrated in the air like a bowstring.

Just in time, the butler, Nigel, reappeared. "Dinner is served, Mrs. Merced."

"Thanks, Nigel." She stood, and Ben rose from his chair. She slid an arm through his and smiled up at him. "Let's go get some food, honey."

In the massive dining room, Ben held a chair for Anastasia and then sat next to her as she instructed, with Remy, not Alan beside him. Alan was seated across the table beside Trudy.

Anastasia said, "I split you up from your intended since I want you to talk to Remy as well as John Jack. I keep tellin' these boys that we need to do more in the way of corporate responsibility. People forgave us for keeping all the moola for ourselves when we were still building, but now it's just plain selfish-looking. Who better to tell us where to contribute a pile of dough than a friend of the family, so to speak?"

Ben's heart leaped, but when he got a "significant" look from Alan, his stomach moved in the opposite direction.

The butler and a maid began serving soup. When all the dishes were distributed, Alan said, "I think it's great that you want Ben to make the company look good, Anastasia, but while you're at it, would you tell him he can lighten up now? This guy works eighty hours a week, and he doesn't have to. Hell, he's going to be an Ashland. Nobody needs his salary, and I don't want an absentee husband."

John Jack raised his glass—another highball rather than the white wine the rest of them drank with their lobster bisque. "Damned right. Relax and enjoy, man."

Ben stared into his soup, trying to ignore the silence that descended over the table.

Anastasia said, "How do you feel about that, Ben?"

He looked up and met her eyes. "I like to work." He took another mouthful of soup. It didn't taste as good as it had.

A few beats of empty air followed his statement, and then Anastasia growled, "Damned right."

Ben's head snapped up.

She grinned at him. "Who the fuck cares how much you make if you do work you love? Nobody ever gave me and Billy Ray a dime. We loved makin' every dollar of our fortune, and I'd never trust a dollar of it to some yahoo who wants to play tennis on a Wednesday. Hard work hones the character, my momma used to say." She waved her spoon at Alan. "You should be proud you've got a man who wants to work for a living and hire yourself somebody to do the rest."

Alan frowned, but the salad replaced the soup at that moment, and he shut up.

Remy turned to him. "So I'm very anxious to know what you think would be the best use of our contribution."

Ben said, "I actually brought a whole presentation that my staff worked hard to put together for you, so I'll be killed if I don't show it."

"Far be it from me to be responsible for your death." Remy held up his hands and laughed. "So what do you do for fun outside of those eighty working hours?"

Alan burst out, "He doesn't do anything!" He leaned across the table toward Anastasia. "You can't tell me that Billy Ray didn't expect you to be available to entertain his clients."

She turned to him slowly, and this time she didn't even try to smile. "Honey, Billy Ray didn't get to *expect* me to do diddly shit. I made way more than half of that money. What do you think, that I'm some trophy wife? I took my clients to dinner. He took his. Sometimes we met up. We saw each other often enough to get two kids." She sat back. "Ben's here because we just might give a lot of money to the things he cares about and works so hard for. Tonight *you're* the trophy wife." She brayed a laugh at her own joke. "So let's finish this food and see what Ben brought for us."

Alan forced a smile and started talking to John Jack. Remy seemed happy to make social conversation with Ben, and Ben responded, but everything felt like fingernails on the blackboard. All he could think about was Dusty—how he looked having that seizure, his dreamy, confused eyes afterward, and how angry and upset he'd been with Ben in the hall before the seizure. *No way around it, I caused the seizure. I brought it on. I upset him so badly by practically attacking him, he broke down.* Ben blinked.

"Ben? Are you okay?"

"What?" He glanced at Anastasia, who smiled at him with a cocked head. Jesus, he almost sat there and cried.

Terrific, on the brink of the biggest presentation he'd ever given. "Yes, sorry. Just kind of worried, uh, about my friend."

"I can imagine. Let's get this dog-and-pony on the road so you can get back to him." She pushed away from the table and stood. "Nigel, how about we have dessert in the living room in a few minutes? People can freshen up, and we'll hear what Ben has to say."

Everyone stood, and Anastasia walked over to Ben and slid an arm through his again. "Come on, honey." She walked him into the living room as the others milled about, went to the bathroom, and chatted. She looked up at him. "What's wrong?"

He released some breath. He really liked this woman, but he should tread lightly. Hell, he didn't know her at all, but he trusted her for some reason. "My friend had an epileptic seizure. I've never seen one before, and it shook me. Plus I didn't know he had epilepsy, and I'm afraid I increased the stress he was under and contributed to his having the seizure."

Holy crap, he'd just spilled the whole thing.

Anastasia frowned, looked toward the dining room, and said, "Hold on, everybody. I need to talk to Ben for a few minutes. We're going back in the den." She pulled his arm. "Come on."

Heat crept up his face. Had he just blown it for all the people Anastasia's money could have helped?

She led him to a big room at the back of the house, with a huge fireplace and a lot of bookshelves. Closing the door, she pointed to one of the couches. "Sit."

He sat.

Anastasia perched on a chair upholstered in fabric covered with ducks. "What do you know about my daddy?"

What? "Nothing much. I know you were very poor when you met your husband and still you married for love, not money. That suggests to me your family might have been happy despite not having a pot to piss in, as they say. That's just a feeling."

"It's an accurate feeling. I'm from the hills of Arkansas. My daddy worked construction, but it was damned hard for him to make ends meet. Know why?"

Ben shrugged. "Inconsistent work, low wages in Arkansas?"

"Because he had epilepsy."

"Well, hell."

"Yep. Couldn't get insurance. When he could afford medication, it slowed his seizures but made him depressed and forgetful. The stress of trying to raise me and take care of my mom just kept him in a cycle."

Ben shook his head. "Honestly, I knew so little about the disorder until today."

"You got an in-your-face introduction."

"Yes, ma'am."

"I gather this friend matters to you."

Ben glanced at his hands, then back up into her knowing gray eyes. "Uh, he's a relatively new friend, but yes."

She just stared at him, then suddenly stood. "Come on."

Like he'd boarded his own flying carpet, they whizzed back down the hall to the living room, where everyone was chowing down on what looked like chocolate cheesecake.

"Okay, we're back. Ben, sit while I tell these critters how it's going to be."

Once again, he sat.

"Ben and I have discussed it, and I propose we donate twenty-five million to epilepsy research in honor of my daddy. Ben and his people will administer the funds and find appropriate recipients. In addition, I'm asking that Ben take on Trudy as a member of his staff."

John Jack flew out of his chair while Trudy just looked amazed—and delighted. John Jack sputtered, "What?"

Anastasia waved a hand. "Oh, come on. I hate to see a good brain being wasted. Especially a female brain. And I know Trudy will be an asset. Plus she'll watch out for our assets." She laughed. "Like that idea, Trudy?"

"Yes, ma'am." Trudy beamed.

"Okay. Then we'll throw in another ten mil for Ben and Trudy to use for whatever other worthy causes they feel need it and will enhance the Merced brand." She flashed a crooked smile. "Can't *just* be altruistic here." She sat down in the easy chair and spread her hands on the wide arms. "All in favor, say aye."

Remy raised a hand. "Aye, Mamma, aye."

John Jack scowled as Anastasia said, "The ayes have it." She turned. "Ben, I promise we'll watch your presentation on our own. It'll help get Trudy up to speed. Honest to God, she's got a degree in business and way better mind than most. Now, why don't you get back to your friend, honey?"

Alan frowned. "Friend?"

Ben's heart hammered. *I wish I knew if I had a friend.*

CHAPTER ELEVEN

"Ben. Wait!"

Damn. Almost home free. Ben took a breath as he released the handle of his car door and prepared to turn and greet a pissed-off Alan. *Wish I knew what I want to say.* But he didn't, and unless he had an epiphany in the next two seconds, he'd better face the music as it was. He turned and smiled—slightly. "Hi."

The frown Alan had been wearing for the last half hour as Ben left a copy of the presentation on a memory stick for the Merceds to watch, arranged a meeting time with Trudy, and thanked Anastasia for her amazing generosity, now turned to a scowl. "What do you mean, hi?"

"Come on, Alan. It's been a tough day."

"I gathered. A day built around your *friend* and his problems." Oh man, the word *friend* should have been *hooker*.

"Partly."

Alan crossed his arms. "I gather you got everything you wanted from the evening. Anastasia's money and a whole lot more work to assure you're never available to do anything with me."

Ben spoke softly. "That money will do a lot of good for a lot of people."

"And among those people, I'm the lowest priority."

A flash went off in Ben's brain. "Oh."

Alan didn't hear him. He was on a roll. "We need to set the date, Ben. We need to plan a wedding. Weddings, actually, because Mommy and Daddy want to have a ceremony in Europe for friends there as well as one here. I want to take an extended honeymoon. Maybe a safari, and then lying on the beach in the Seychelles. We need to buy a house and get that monstrosity of yours sold and you moved in with me so we can finally have some fun. Dear God, Ben, when will *our* life begin?"

Ben put a hand on Alan's arm. "Dear, stop." Something like elation bubbled up his throat, and he had to force himself not to laugh. "My life has started, and it looks much like I want it to right now—with a few notable exceptions. I care about you. You're a good man, but I don't want to live your life. It's not a matter of compromise. Our priorities can't be compromised. They'll never go together. You've flattered me with your love and attention. I'm not sure why, but I'm grateful. At the same time, I have to bow out. You need someone who'll appreciate all that you can give them rather than resenting it."

Alan stared at him like he'd lost his mind—and maybe he had. "Are you—?"

"Yes, I'm breaking our engagement, so you'll be free to find someone who'll really make you happy." *And so can I.*

"I thought we made each other happy." He crossed his arms.

"Alan, you want someone who can live your life with joy and enthusiasm. Who wants to go on a safari and have a second wedding in Europe. I'm simply not that person, and if you think I am, you haven't been listening. I love my life as it is." *Well, almost.*

"But you'll change. As soon as you get a taste of the life I can offer—"

"I've had a taste. I genuinely care about you and like you, except when you're trying to turn me into the man of your dreams. I have to live my own dreams, Alan."

Alan's pleading expression morphed into a frown, and he pointed back toward the mansion. "Anastasia will never give you that money if we're not engaged."

Ben sucked a breath. "So be it."

"You're mad."

Ben snorted a laugh. "I know."

Finally knowing what wouldn't make him happy was a blessing. What were his chances of having what did make him happy?

BEN STARED at the phone on his desk like it could bite him. *I've got to know.* He reached out a hand—

"Ben?"

Saved by the admin. "Hi, Mary Kaye."

She grinned. "Uh, I don't want to pressure you, but—" She pressed her hands together. "What happened?"

"I'm about to find out."

"Oh. Holy crap. So they decided to make a decision this morning?"

"Not exactly. It's a long story. Let me make the call before I lose my nerve."

Her eyes widened. "Okay. Shall I close the door?"

"Yeah, you better." *There could be begging.* "And get her on the phone, please." He couldn't trust himself to dial.

She tiptoed backward with big eyes and closed his door

carefully, then pressed her face against the glass of his window like a kitten in a cage.

He laughed… and shuddered. If this went south, he'd let a lot of people down.

His desk phone rang. *Oh man.* He picked it up, inhaled, and pushed the button to connect. "Hi, Anastasia."

"Hi, honey. How you this mornin'? Getting ready to spend all our money?" She laughed.

"About that, I need to tell you something that might influence your decision."

"Oh?"

"Yes. Last night after I saw you, I broke my engagement with Alan. So I'm not going to be family, as you said."

"Holy shit, honey. When did this happen?"

"Frankly, in your driveway after I met with you."

She started to laugh.

What the hell?

She managed to gasp out, "Well, hallelujah. I hope I had something to do with it."

"What? Anastasia, I never would have met you if it weren't for Alan and his family."

She sucked air and controlled her laughter, "Which proves he's served his purpose." She laughed a little more. "Come on, honey, are you trying to talk yourself out of it? I couldn't figure out what you were doing with that self-entitled twerp in the first place."

"Really?" Air was flooding back into his lungs, making him light-headed.

"He's not as bad as John Jack, but that'd be true condemnation. No worries, honey. Just let us know when and where we need to send the money. I'll make the arrangements on this end. We're honored to have you and ClearWater responsible for our contributions."

"Thank you, Anastasia." God, he could pass out from hyperventilation. "Do you want to be involved in the selection of the charities and researchers who receive the epilepsy funds?"

"I'll tell Trudy what I want and what to look for."

"I look forward to working with her."

"You'll love her, honey. One of the few smart personal decisions John Jack ever made. He just doesn't know it. He's a good businessman, though, so don't worry about him fighting us on this."

"Okay."

"He's not really a misogynist. He just acts like one." She chuckled. "He's scared of women. I guess I was too much for him growing up. Still am. But it's funny. He thought he was marrying a bimbo, but his innate intelligence got him hooked to one of the smartest females around."

Ben chuckled.

"By the way, if you're lookin' for a new boyfriend, I've got a feeling Remy might have a queer bent to him."

"Anastasia, you're a yenta."

"I've been called worse. So no go, huh?"

"I'm sorting out my feelings. I'm barely out of my engagement."

"Um-hm. So what about that friend of yours? How's he doing?"

"Uh, I don't know. I have to call this morning." The butterflies roared back like F-18s.

"Why don't you use him as an epilepsy expert? He can help you out better than any of us can."

"That's an amazing idea."

"Yep, I think so. So what does he do for a living?"

"He's a college student and a handyman."

She laughed low. "You robbin' the cradle there, honey?"

"Oh no. I mean, he's twenty-three and poor and it's taking him time to go to school and—Jesus, he's not my boyfriend."

"Yeah, having epilepsy in our fucked-up healthcare system is no small burden. I know firsthand. I'm lucky neither of my boys got it. So give this man a good job helping other people like him. On me, okay?"

He wanted to drop his head to the desk and bawl in amazed gratitude. "I don't know how to thank you."

"Just do a good job for us. We'll be PRing the shit out of this contribution, don't think we won't."

"Anything I can do to shine the image of Merced Enterprises is at your disposal, ma'am." He said it with a drawl, and she laughed.

"By the way, honey, about that boyfriend thing. You doth protest too much, methinks." She laughed raucously. "Now aren't you surprised I know my Shakespeare?"

He shook his head. "Anastasia, I wouldn't be surprised if you could recite the *Iliad* in Greek."

"Ask me next week. You get on with your life, honey. Let me know how I can help. I loved my husband and I'm a hopeless romantic. See ya."

She hung up, and he stared at the phone.

The door opened. "Hi. I was watching through the window. You don't look devastated—exactly."

He raised his eyes and let his head follow as he smiled.

She clapped her hands. "Tell me! Tell me."

"Twenty-five million for epilepsy research and another ten mil for any other projects we recommend."

"Epilepsy? Really?"

"Anastasia's father had it."

"No shit?"

"And we're about to have two new employees. Anastasia wants us to hire her daughter-in-law, Trudy, to help administer the Merced money and whatever else we want to do with her."

"A family spy in our midst?" Mary Kaye grinned.

"Actually, I think she'll be an asset."

"And who's the other one?"

Ben chewed his lip. "Dusty."

"You're joking."

"Nope. Me telling Anastasia about Dusty's seizure last night is what inspired the whole donation."

Mary Kaye leaned against the doorjamb. "Well, I'll be damned." She frowned for a second. "You know, that's a pretty incredible idea. He's bright, capable, and knows the subject personally."

Ben nodded. Making that happen had one giant obstacle. Dusty.

His venomous business phone had become a many-headed hydra. He didn't want to call Dusty on his cell since that might imply a personal request. That would be bad. *Oh shit, I'm more nervous than when I called Anastasia.*

The tap on his door suggested some cosmic conspiracy to keep him from making scary phone calls. "Yes?"

The door opened, and Craig stepped in. "Hey." He grinned, since Ben had called him and told him about the Merced donation.

"Hi."

Craig closed the door and suddenly it pushed open again as Mary Kaye bounded through. "Sorry. I know I've got no rank in this room, but I do have opinions."

Ben cocked his head. "When was that ever not true? Sit, both of you." His phone rang. He raised a finger and mouthed *the boss*. "Yes, James." James Tilden had founded

ClearWater and remained its dynamic, entrepreneurial CEO.

"Ben, wow. I mean, fantastic. Anastasia Merced? With her behind the foundation, you're going to be beating donors off with a stick. We'll be able to save the world."

"So let it be done."

James laughed. "I'm proud of you and the whole team."

"Marketing did an amazing job on this. Practically overnight." He'd never say he didn't even get to show the presentation.

"Tell Craig congratulations, and I'll say that myself as soon as I get back from India."

"Is that where you are?" He widened his eyes.

"Yeah. Just got back from one of those eternal dinners. Fun but hard on the digestion. I'm going to need a gallon of wheatgrass to get me in shape."

"Oh man, you're such a Californian."

"Yep, get me back to the land of the fruits and the nuts, my friend."

"I reckon I'm both."

"In the best way. See you soon." He hung up.

Craig said, "Sounds like James is happy."

"Yeah."

Craig looked at Mary Kaye uneasily. He must want to talk about Dusty or Alan or something.

Mary Kaye glanced over at Craig, sat back in her chair, and sighed. "Okay, you guys. I've figured out all on my own that Ben has some kind of crush on Dusty Kincaid. That's why I'm here. I just wanted to say I don't think you should let this Merced deal make you stay with a man you don't love. I don't care if James wants to gold plate your dick, it's not worth it to wreck your life to be with the wrong person. Dump your so-called fiancé and tell Dusty you care about him."

Well, damn. Ben chuckled. "I broke the engagement last night. That's why I was so nervous this morning. I had to call Anastasia and tell her."

"Yeehaw! What'd she say?"

"Something like it was about time." He flashed the dimples.

"There, you see? She didn't get to be that rich by being dumb."

"But—" Craig made a circular motion with his hand.

"She suggested the foundation should hire Dusty as an expert." Ben inhaled. "Now I just need to call him and ask him." He stared daggers at the phone.

Mary Kaye said, "Do you think that's wise?"

"What?"

She shrugged. "I heard what he said to you in the hall."

"Jesus, did everyone in the company hear it?"

"Pretty much. Anyway, if you call, Dusty's going to think it's charity. Why doesn't Craig call and offer him the job?"

Craig shook his head. "I don't work for the foundation, and Dusty probably knows that. Maybe HR could call."

"Wait." Mary Kaye's pixie face lit up. "I've got an idea."

Dusty sat on the bus bench listening to Chopin and staring at his hands. He'd escaped philosophy class and had an hour to get to the health food restaurant where he could have his lunch before he started work. Philosophy usually captivated him. Today, not so much. *I think, therefore I am* was clearly ridiculous. *I love, therefore I am* made way more sense. But if you loved and didn't get loved back, did that mean you weren't?

He let his head fall back. *Jesus, get over yourself. Descartes doesn't need your help. More like I should go write scripts for* Days of Our Lives.

He didn't usually feel sorry for himself, and he'd be damned if he'd start now. Still, it was hard to feel alive with a big hole in his heart. Sadly, a lot of his memory had come back, and the moments before he had the seizure stood out in bas relief. Ben didn't want him. Ben had a rich, gorgeous fiancé, so why the hell would he need a good morning from Dusty?

Drama queen! He jumped up, paced to a tree across the sidewalk, and slammed a hand against the smooth, bumpy eucalyptus trunk. *Ow.*

His phone rang. *What?* His mom knew where he was. Jesus, she'd hardly let him breathe since he had the seizure.

The screen said ClearWater. Oh man, he'd been trying to get up enough nerve to call and quit. But he didn't want to. A third ring pierced the air, and a woman sitting on the bench waiting for the bus glanced at him. Oh hell, might as well. He answered just as the phone stopped ringing.

Oh. Okay, he should call HR and tell them. What? That his school schedule changed? Nah, they'd just try to rearrange his hours. *I should say I got another job. Yeah.* He sighed long and painfully. They'd been so good to him, paying more than the position really deserved and giving him interesting assignments whenever they came up. He liked everyone there so much.

So much.

Maybe I should call and say I'm in love with the vice president in charge of your foundation. How's that for workplace fraternization? That'd get him fired in a red-hot minute. Of course, it took two to fraternize. He smiled at the thought.

Wow, he'd go from having too many jobs to not enough in one day. No ClearWater. No Ben's house. That last part made him want to grab his chest. *Stop. You can't do this to yourself again. Calm down.* But the truth was he'd have to move fast finding a new job. His mom didn't like to admit it, but she relied on his income to survive.

The bus came around the corner, and he walked back across the sidewalk as it approached the stop.

His phone rang. *Damn.* Talking on the bus was so rude. He stared at the screen. The woman next to him gave him a look, then climbed on the bus. *Message received.* He clicked the phone off and went up the stairs after her.

CHAPTER TWELVE

"Damn. Why doesn't he answer?" Ben looked up at Mary Kaye, hovering conspiratorially in his doorway—as usual.

She shook her head. "I've tried three times. The last time it went straight to voicemail. I really thought if he saw a Clear-Water number, he'd answer."

"Me too. Maybe he's at work or in class and can't take calls?"

"Probably."

He nodded. *Try not to look like the entire fate of the world depends on this call.* Of course, reaching Dusty didn't mean shit. All he had to say was no.

Mary Kaye grinned. Not fooled.

"Keep trying." He made a shooing gesture, and she laughed and left the office. He worked at appearing like he was working. At least investigating epilepsy researchers was interesting enough to keep him from totally wasting the time.

His phone rang, and he jumped a foot. *Cell phone. Calm down.* Ben's mom. Yes, he had been avoiding her. He sighed and answered. "Hey, Mom."

"I'm sorry to bother you at work, dear, but I didn't expect

you to fall off the grid after the party." Yes, it was a motherly accusation, but she said it with a smile in her voice, at least.

"Sorry, Mom. A lot's happened."

"Yes, I'm sure. But your father and I need to know if the wedding venue is going to be local, because we'd like to hold a party for your friends since I know that Alan's family parties will be mostly strangers and—"

"Whoa! Hold on, Mom." How had he let her get so far behind? In his defense, it had been just a few days. "Are you sitting down?"

"Why?"

"Because I need to tell you that I broke the engagement, and I don't want you to hit your head when you faint."

Silence, like a tidal wave pouring from his family home toward him.

"I'm sorry, Mom. I know you wanted this for me, but I just can't do it. Alan's great and I cared about him, but what you and Dad taught me by example was really different than what you wanted for me. You dreamed of me having everything handed to me, while you guys worked your butts off and enjoyed doing it. I can't become an ornament and defend the things I care about every day of my life. Alan's great, but he has a particular kind of life he wants to live, and it's just not my life. I don't want to plan parties and lie on beaches. I want a partner with the same kind of passion I have for something." Dusty flashed in his mind. *Whoa. Take a step back.*

"Oh my."

"Mom, you can't tell me you felt comfortable with the Ashlands and their friends."

"No, dear, I didn't. But I thought you did."

"I'm my parents' son."

"We're very, very proud of you, Ben."

"Thank you."

"And if I'm honest, I wanted the money for you more than the man."

"I understand. It wasn't easy to walk away from that much luxury and ease."

She made a snorting sound. "Yes, it was. When did you ever care about money unless it was being donated to save something?"

"Speaking of which, Anastasia Merced—remember, who I met at the party?"

"She's unforgettable."

"She and her sons are giving the foundation... hold your breath."

"I'm holding." She giggled.

"Thirty-five million."

"Holy crap."

He laughed. "Squared."

"All right, dear. I'll break the news to your father that he won't be playing golf with POTUS—which he never wanted to do one tiny bit."

"Thanks, Mom. Let's go out to dinner soon."

"No, you come here."

"I'd love to." He kissed into the phone and she kissed back, an artifact from childhood he still loved.

As he clicked off, he stared into space. One more hurdle, and it was huge.

DUSTY SNIFFED his hands. Wheatgrass. He smelled like a new-mown lawn. Slowly he walked toward the bus stop. Tired. The lump of the phone in his pocket bounced against his hip. *Damn.* He'd forgotten to turn it back on after the bus. His mom might have called. He pulled it out of his pocket and clicked. It took a few seconds to boot up, and then he input his passcode.

Like the thing came to life, it began to ring. *Whoa!* He clicked it and pressed it to his ear. "I'm on my way home."

A pause. "Is this Dusty Kincaid?"

He glanced at the phone. *Well, damn. ClearWater.* "Sorry, I thought you were someone else."

"Dusty, my name is Trudy Merced."

"Yes, ma'am." A new name, but ClearWater hired a lot of people in HR. "I'm sorry, I've been meaning to call you."

"Me?"

"Well, HR."

"I'm not with HR, Dusty. But I would like to speak to you about a job opportunity. Is there a chance you could come in to ClearWater during your regular shift tomorrow?"

No way could he quit on the spot and leave them hanging. Maybe they had more shelves for him to build. "Yes, ma'am."

She laughed softly. "That's excellent, Dusty. How about 9:00 a.m.? Just ask for Trudy at the front desk."

"Yes, ma'am."

"And can you call me Trudy too?"

"Okay." *Wow.*

"See you tomorrow."

For a half hour, he tried to listen to Chopin and not think of Ben. Yes, stupid concept. Who had introduced him to Chopin? But he couldn't bring himself to stop listening. It soothed him in a sappy, gut-wrenching way.

Finally he dragged himself off the bus and slowly walked the five blocks home.

Inside, he smelled food. His mom called, "Hi. Are you hungry?"

He knew better than to say no. "Starving."

"Go change. It will be ready in a minute."

He walked to his bedroom, closed the door, and sat on the

bed. *Trudy. Who is she?* He was excited to talk to her and scared to see Ben, but he was scared shitless he wouldn't get to see him.

He flopped back on the bed and closed his eyes. That beautiful hair that could look brown until the light shone on it, and then it flamed to life. The eyes. The ass. He chuckled. Oh man, he remembered what that butt felt like under his hands.

Stop! He sat up and started stripping his clothes. Terrific idea to daydream about Ben when Dusty had no chance of ever being with him. And even if some fairy waved a wand and made Dusty irresistible to Ben, he'd have no right to be with him. Hell, Dusty would be like an anchor on the beautiful shooting star that was Ben. Ben had a rich, gorgeous fiancé, just like he deserved.

The tap on the door made him grab for his jeans and sweatshirt. "Coming, Mom."

"Are you decent?"

"Will be in a second." He pulled on the jeans commando and yanked the shirt over his head, then opened the door.

His mom stood outside the door, her face carefully composed to look pleasant. Not a good sign. "What's up?"

"Uh, kind of bad news, but nothing we can't handle." She smiled.

"What?"

"You know how we've wondered what would happen to the house now that the kids own it?"

He nodded. *Damn.*

"Well, they're selling it, so we need to find a new place. I've been looking online."

"How long do we have?"

She sighed as they walked toward the kitchen. "That's the other bad news. They've only given us two weeks."

"Wow."

"I know. I didn't want to tell you, but there's so little time, I—"

"Of course, you needed to tell me."

"I've already taken a load of my old clothes to the Goodwill." She started filling their plates.

As if all her clothes weren't old. "I'll start looking tomorrow."

"Okay. I've pulled a lot of shifts at the hospital, which is good since we'll need a deposit, but that means you'll have to do a lot of the looking." She put the plates on their small table next to his glass of water.

"Not a problem. You know how I love snooping in houses." Finding anything they could afford would be another matter. Real estate prices were climbing in Orange County again, which meant people couldn't afford to buy, so they rented, and that pushed up rental prices. Vicious cycle. *Don't look stressed.* He tried to look at least moderately composed and picked up his fork.

Because she watched his every mouthful, he managed to get about half the mac and cheese, broccoli, and salad into his mouth. He leaned back. "I ate at work, so I'm pretty full."

She stared at him like she could see how many calories he'd consumed. "Okay, but I made you some peanut butter celery for later." She rose and started clearing. He grabbed his plate, but she stopped him. "Go watch some TV. You need to rest."

"Thanks, Mom." He walked into the small living room as she cleared the table.

She said, "Did you quit ClearWater?"

"Uh, no. A funny thing happened. I got a call from this woman saying they had a job for me. I felt like I couldn't just quit and leave them hanging, so I'll tell them after I finish whatever this job is."

"Any idea what they want you to do?"

"No. Probably more shelves or something."

"Don't tire yourself out."

He frowned. "I like to work. It helps me. And they pay me extra for special projects, so I appreciate your concern—" He gritted his teeth.

"You appreciate it but butt out?"

"Yes, ma'am."

"Okay, Dusty. I'm sorry. It's hard for me not to treat you like my baby."

"I know." He smiled. "You're forgiven. Plus we're going to need whatever money I can scrape together for this move."

"Don't think that way. I'll be able to manage everything with the extra shifts." She turned on the water in the sink and conversation got hard.

He clicked on the TV. He didn't really want to watch it, but it made his mom think he was relaxing.

His phone dinged. *What the heck?*

"Is that your phone?" she called from the kitchen.

"Just work with times." He opened his text and looked.

Hi Dusty, it's Mary Kaye. I'm looking forward to seeing you.

He stared at the screen. *Why did she text me? Does Ben know? Jesus, I need to quit, but how can I?* Black spots danced in front of his eyes, and he squeezed them shut and breathed deeply.

"Dusty, what's wrong?" His mom hurried over, wiping her hands on a towel.

"Oh, nothing. Just a little tired." His thumb clicked the phone button. "Maybe I should go to bed since I have to work tomorrow."

"Are you all right?"

"Sure. Fine." He rose and kissed her cheek, then walked firmly to the bedroom. He flopped on the bed and stared at the ceiling. *What the hell's going on?*

"Hey, Dusty, how you doing?"

Dusty nodded at the receptionist. Answering that question would take about a year. "Hi, Genevieve. I'm supposed to ask for Trudy."

"Oh right. The new person. I'll call her."

Dusty wandered over to the grouping of chairs. Last time he'd been in this lobby, he'd been writhing on the floor. *Damn. As soon as I talk to Trudy, I'll go to HR and quit. Maybe I can get some more time at the restaurant or even go back to construction.*

He sat and dropped his head in his hand.

"Dusty?"

He looked up at a tall, blond, gorgeous woman and leaped to his feet. "Sorry."

"You okay?"

"Oh, yes, ma'am. Trudy."

She laughed, a pretty, low laugh. "Well, good. Come on." He followed her into the inner offices that he could have gotten into on his own since he had a maintenance key, but he felt positively executive walking beside her. Of course, his threadbare jeans and T-shirt didn't contribute to the image.

The second he entered the inner offices, his eyes started darting around on their own. *A glimpse. Just one. From a distance.*

"In here, please."

"What? Oh, thank you." He followed her into a small

conference room. He'd emptied the trash in there lots of times.

"Please." She pointed to a chair and sat across from him at the round table. "Dusty, I want to talk to you about a job."

He smiled. "More shelves?"

"What?" She frowned. "No. We're asking you to work for the foundation."

"What?" Was she making fun of him? "I don't understand."

"We'd like to offer you a position as an executive assistant for the foundation."

His heart wrenched, and he frowned. "I can't do that."

"Oh? Do you already have a position?"

She seemed serious. "No, I don't have the skills to work for the foundation. I'm a not-yet-educated handyman." What was this woman doing? "Does Ben know you're talking to me?" He stood. "I'm surprised that he'd do this."

She stood next to him. Really tall. "Dusty, please sit down." He sat and stared at his hands. She said, "Wait here for a minute."

He sighed and nodded. Ben was pitying him. Making work for the fucking invalid. He shook his head.

The door to the side opened, and a different woman walked in. Older, attractive, just as blond, expensively dressed in a denim pantsuit, and with an expression that was friendly but definitely not pitying. Dusty stood.

She stuck out a hand. "Dusty, I'm Anastasia Merced. Ever heard of me?"

He bit his tongue to keep from saying *holy shit*. "Yes, ma'am. Retail, technology, environmental science, and a lot more."

"Right. Sit."

Man, did he sit.

She sat next to him. "One thing I never did do was give my money away, and I'm changing that. I've asked the Clear-Water Foundation to administer a large donation from Merced Enterprises."

Dusty swallowed. Of course, Ben must have met her through his fiancé. *That's going to be such a good marriage for Ben. Two of a kind.* "That's a wise decision, ma'am. No one will treat your money more wisely or with more respect than Ben Shane, uh, and his team."

"I agree." She leaned back and stared at him levelly. "One thing you don't know is my daddy had epilepsy."

"Really?"

"Yes, and it fucked up his life royally. On the medication, he didn't get seizures, but he was a zombie. Off the medication, he had too many seizures to function. Health insurance crapped out, and me and my momma worked night and day to keep our family alive. That's where I learned to work."

Dusty realized he was nodding his head like a loon and stopped. "I understand."

"I know you do—on all fronts. You know what it's like to live with epilepsy, you're disciplined about trying to deal with it, and you work your ass off to keep you and your mom moving ahead."

"She does a lot."

"I know that too."

"Did Ben tell you all this?" He frowned.

"Yes. The day you had the seizure, he was scheduled to come and present his program to me and my sons. He knew our meeting was worth millions to his foundation, but he was an hour late because he didn't want to leave you. He later told me why and told me about you."

"I see."

"That's why I want you working for me, Dusty."

"What?"

She waved a hand. "I know you don't have your degree yet. Neither did Steve Jobs."

Dusty snorted, and she grinned at him. He smiled. "Uh, Mrs. Merced, I don't want to oversell here."

"It's okay. I'm not looking for Apple. But you have experience no one else does. I'm contributing millions to epilepsy research." He sucked in a breath, and she nodded. "Right. One in twenty-six people in this country has it. We need some answers. I want you to quit whatever other jobs you have, increase your class schedule if you feel up to it, and work for the foundation with my daughter-in-law, Trudy, guided by Ben and his staff."

He swallowed and breathed, trying hard to not hyperventilate. In Wikipedia, under Dreams Come True, they posted this job. *Hang on, idiot. Maybe the researchers aren't the only ones getting charity.* "Ma'am, did Ben suggest me for this job?"

"No. I suggested it to him."

He looked up at her.

"He called me brilliant. Seriously, Dusty, do you think I'd contribute thirty-five million dollars and come here today to provide you with a handout?"

Thirty-five million? Holy shit. He cocked a grin. "Maybe."

She exploded a laugh. "If you want to think I'm that charitable, I'll let you. But in this case, I firmly believe you're the right guy for the job. I'll expect all your brains and creativity, and I'll expect you to take care of yourself so you can walk the talk."

"Mrs. Merced, you don't know me at all. You don't even know if I'm smart or creative. All you know is I have epilepsy. Lots of people with more brains and skill than me have it too."

"Yes, but you're in the right place at the right time. You're young, so I can get you cheap and bring you up to suit myself. And, of course, Ben Shane believes in you."

"Why?" The crease between his brows deepened.

"You'll have to ask him. I'm assuming, however, that your own self-doubt isn't enough to make you turn down this job."

Dusty stared into space for a second. *What the hell am I doing?* His gaze snapped up and met hers. "No, ma'am. I mean, yes, I'd be honored and thrilled to accept a position with the foundation. I'll do everything in my power to justify your faith in me."

"I know you will, honey." She stood and he rose beside her. She said, "Get your ducks in a row. You'll be reporting to Trudy, but she's brand-new too, so you'll both be working for whoever Ben says."

He nodded.

She put a warm hand on his shoulder. "Go talk to Ben."

"Why?"

"Because you want to." She smiled and dropped her grasp. "Trudy will be back in and take you to HR."

"Thank you. I mean, for everything."

"We'll be seeing each other."

"I hope so." He stuck out his hand, and she shook it.

"Now that Ben's broken up with his silly fiancé, you can both figure out who you really are. Plus I can have you to dinner—together."

"What? What do you mean, broken up?" Dusty flopped back into the chair.

She popped a hand against her mouth. "Oops." She chuckled as she walked out the door.

CHAPTER THIRTEEN

Ben stared at the computer screen—redux. Honestly, for a man who was supposed to be a workaholic, he'd sure put in a lot of fruitless hours recently. But his body tingled like a neon sign flashing *Dusty. Dusty. Dusty.* He was here somewhere and—

His office door opened and closed. Slowly, Ben raised his eyes. *Wow. Just Wow.* Dusty in his blue T-shirt and those jeans that always hugged exactly where they should hug. "You look nice." He dropped his head into his hand. "If you wait a minute I might be able to find some other totally lame thing to say."

"No, I look stupid since I thought I was coming in to build shelves." He ran his hands down his thighs, which only made Ben's own thighs tense. Dusty sighed. "You broke your engagement."

Ben looked up. "Yes."

"Why?"

"Because I didn't love him and didn't want the life he offered." He held up a hand. "Don't misunderstand. I thought I cared about him enough to marry him for a while because—"

He shrugged. "—I had so little basis for comparison." He stared into those blue, blue eyes where he'd like to drown. "I would have told you, but I didn't want you to think that was some kind of invitation or ultimatum or come-on. You know?"

"Was it?"

"What?"

"An invitation?" Dusty crossed his well-muscled arms and frowned, which on his sweet face looked scary and funny at the same time.

"Uh, absolutely."

"What kind?"

"How about dinner?"

"I can't date you. I'm your employee."

"You are?" Ben grinned, and it spread across his face like peanut butter.

"Hell, you sent the richest woman in the world to talk me into it."

"I didn't send her, and I've got news for you. That doesn't stop me from taking you to dinner. There's no antifraternization policy in this company. James Tilden married his admin, and he's not a hypocrite." He swallowed. "But just because I can ask doesn't mean you have to say yes."

Dusty finally walked to a chair and sat. All the irate self-assurance that apparently propelled him in there seemed to drain away. "Why are you doing this for me?"

"What?" Ben frowned. "I'm not doing anything *for* you." Ben stood and stalked to the corner of his office, then back. "What in the hell do you think this is? Me trying to seduce some"—he threw his arms out—"child? I know I'm six years older, but come on, that's not a lifetime. Yes, I've got more professional experience, but you've got more life experience, and we both have things to teach each other. I totally understand if you don't want to go out with me, but don't make up some shit story about how I feel sorry for you."

"You don't?" Dusty looked up with dimples popping.

"No."

Dusty rose and sauntered a few steps to where Ben stood. "You don't even feel sorry about the fact that every time I see you, I want to jump your bones?"

Ben put a hand on Dusty's cheek. "Didn't that expression go out in the seventies?"

Dusty shrugged. "I figured that way you'd recognize it."

Ben snorted. "You realize that while my door's closed, I have giant windows out to the hall."

"Yes. I first saw you through those windows, sitting behind your desk looking serious and sexy."

"Sexy, huh?"

"Well, you were staring at my ass, so it was hard not to notice you."

"You devil." He moved his hand from Dusty's cheek and ran his fingers through his golden hair. "So will you have dinner with me?"

"When?"

"Well, if we go tonight, you won't actually work for me yet."

"I thought that didn't matter." He cocked his head.

"It doesn't, but if it gets me a faster date, I'm playing the card."

Dusty sighed. "I'm such a boring date. No alcohol, no sugar." He gazed up through his lashes, then stared at the floor. "It doesn't happen much, but I can have a seizure when I have sex."

Oh man. Come on, you want to be with a guy who has epilepsy. Deal with it. "Just tell me what to do if it happens."

He cleared his throat. "I mean, if we ever have sex in the future."

Dusty smiled hesitantly. "Are you sure?"

"Yes. I'm sure." And he was.

Dusty whispered, "Have I mentioned that I give a mean blowjob?" As Ben's jaw fell open, Dusty stepped back. "I have to go to HR now." He winked and walked out the door.

Ben's erection didn't go down for the rest of the day.

BEN TOOK a breath and knocked on the door. Dusty said he'd explain everything to his mom, but maybe she'd be meeting Ben with a gun.

The door opened, and suddenly he didn't care if a hostile herd of alligators waited in that living room. In front of him was a treasure worth braving the rapids for. He snorted at his mixed metaphors.

Dusty stood there in a white shirt, slim black slacks, and a denim jacket. His golden hair shone, and he looked so freshly shaved he practically squeaked. Ben whispered, "Holy crap, you clean up well."

Dusty grinned. "Not so bad yourself." He raised his voice. "Come on in and say hi to my mom."

Into the valley of death. Ben walked into the living room. Mrs. Kincaid sat on the couch, working to hold herself together. *Just do it.* Ben walked straight to her and sat on a chair beside her. "Mrs. Kincaid, I really want Dusty to work for my foundation. It's a job for which he's uniquely qualified. He'll be making a huge contribution to solving some of the major problems of people with epilepsy. It'll also allow him to reduce stress and make more money."

"How will taking on this kind of job reduce his stress?" She spit the words at him.

"He'll only have to have one job. He can work on something absorbing and challenging, but not so physically demanding. He won't spend half his day on the bus, and he'll be able to take more classes if he wants to. He'll also have enough money to afford a more comfortable place for you to live, uh, should you require it."

She narrowed her eyes at him. "And what about you?"

"I care about Dusty. A lot. I'll work with you to be sure he doesn't overdo it. That he gets enough rest and the right food. Hopefully we'll be learning new things that will make his life even easier."

"Do you have any idea what it's like to live with a person who has epilepsy?"

"No." He glanced up into Dusty's frowning face. "But I'd like to find out."

She glared at him. "You're a do-gooder with a savior complex."

"No. I'll be the first to admit that I like making the world a better place, but I have a comfortable life. I don't even have a rescue dog." He smiled. "Of course, I'd like to get Dusty a therapy dog. They seem to be having some luck using dogs with epilepsy patients."

"Mom, I want this job. It's like a dream." Dusty glanced at Ben, then sat next to his mother and took her hand. "And I want to be with Ben. I've never cared for anyone so much. Except you, but that's different." He grinned.

Ben smiled so big his cheeks hurt. Could he even keep his heart in his chest?

Dusty spoke earnestly. "I know you're worried. Hell, so am I, but I can't spend my whole life being afraid. Fear makes me an invalid way more than epilepsy."

Those words seemed to register with her, and her frown relaxed a little. "I know I try to protect you too much." She looked at Ben. "But you weren't there to hold a small boy in your arms while he shook and thrashed, blood dripping from his chewed-up tongue."

"But, Mom, I'm getting better. You know I am. And it's mostly because of you. You've taken such good care of me." He pressed her hand to his cheek. "And you've taught me to take care of myself. I get to have a life because you made it possible."

"No, Dusty. You made it possible." She took a breath. "And you're going to be amazing at helping others learn to live fully with epilepsy. Ben couldn't have found anyone better."

"Thank you, Mom."

She looked up. "Where are you going to dinner?"

Ben said, "I thought we'd try a fish restaurant." He grinned. "Wild caught, of course."

"Salmon is very good for him." She held up a hand. "Sorry. Get going before the restaurant fills up." She wiped a hand across her cheek.

Ben and Dusty stood and walked to the front door. Mrs. Kincaid said, "Ben, make sure he gets enough sleep."

"Yes. I will."

They stepped outside and closed the door. Ben looked at Dusty. "What do you think she meant by that?"

Dusty laughed and took his hand as they walked to the car. Inside, Ben looked over at Dusty, whose hair shone in the soft light from the street. "Do you really care for me more than anyone?"

"Nah, I just said that for her."

Ben's heart flipped.

Dusty leaned across the console and took Ben's chin. "Of course it's true. I'd never say that unless it was. I looked through that big window in your office one early morning and thought the sun had come up inside. You were like my dream all enclosed in a glass box I felt like I'd never be able to open. I can't believe I'm here with you." He leaned over and kissed Ben softly, his warm lips lingering. "Wow. Our first kiss, if you don't count one very wild roll on the bed." He frowned. "Why did you stop that day?"

Ben sighed gently and touched Dusty's face. "I knew I didn't have any right to have you. I was engaged to someone else. I felt like I'd lured you to my house under false pretenses and I was taking advantage of you."

"Don't you remember? I came there on my own. You didn't invite me. I thought I'd taken advantage of you. Lured you into my web with a mop."

"Maybe that's how we'll celebrate our anniversaries. Mopping floors in honor of the first time we almost had sex." Ben started the car. "Hungry?"

"Kind of."

Ben flipped on Chopin and played it very softly as they drove.

As they approached a light on Katella, Dusty said, "Ben?"

"Um-hm?"

"Do you think we can more than almost?"

"What?"

"Have sex?"

Ben sucked air, and he had to slam his foot on the brake to keep from running into the car stopped in front of him.

Dusty giggled. "That got your attention."

"Uh, yes."

"Yes, it got your attention or yes, you want to have sex?"

"Both."

"Well, I haven't inspected your house for a few days."

Ben had to grip the wheel to keep his hands from shaking. "Oh no, your mom will kill me if I don't feed you properly."

"Takeout's good."

"Whoa." The word moaned out on a long column of air. "Don't you want to date for a while? Get to know me first?" He couldn't seem to swallow.

"Hi. I'm Dustin Kincaid. People call me Dusty. I'm going to be twenty-four at the end of June. Epilepsy's slowed me down a little, but I've got big dreams, and you're a part of them. I've wanted you since the first time I ever saw you. I'm a bottom but I'll switch, and I'm happy to have you any way you want, including upside down. Let's have sex."

Ben laughed, and it relieved a few butterflies. "If you promise to eat."

"Oh yes, I do promise to eat."

"Oh God, oh God, oh!"

Ben's head thrashed back on the comforter they'd spread on the floor in the guest room, surrounded by the paper plates and leftovers from their health-food restaurant carryout. Dusty hadn't been kidding about eating. He'd downed a big helping of vegetarian lasagna and salad, and now he was swallowing Ben's cock for dessert.

After a full year of unsatisfying sex, this was like a whole new deal. An amazing, soul-satisfying, heart-expanding revelation.

Suddenly Dusty pulled back. "Where are your supplies?"

"What? Oh, in the bedside table in the master. I mean, that was in the master. Now it's in the hall." He took a breath. Dusty had told him if he had a seizure, just keep him from hitting his head and let him have it. *Okay, then.*

Dusty grasped Ben's penis like a flagpole. "Here. Hold this."

Ben was still laughing when Dusty ran back in with a box

of condoms and a tube of lube. He knelt beside Ben's half-nude body and started removing his own clothes.

Oh man. Ben licked his lips and watched, because Dusty unveiling his body to Ben for the first time was something he knew he'd never forget. Inch after inch of creamy skin crept into view. Dusty didn't seem to be purposefully teasing, but it sure looked that way. First he caught one arm and his head in the white shirt he tried to take off without unbuttoning it. Beautiful fail. By the time he undid enough buttons to get the thing off, his other hand was unfastening his waistband and fly, showing off a V of blue cotton mounded exquisitely over something hard and straining.

Ben wet his lips.

The shirt flew toward the chair, already piled with clothes, and Dusty pulled at his slacks, but he'd only gotten one shoe off, and the pants covered the other one like a tangled hairball.

Ben couldn't help it. He laughed.

Dusty gave him a raised golden eyebrow, and that made Ben laugh harder. His dick didn't exactly think waiting was funny, and it kept bouncing like an online ad trying to get their attention. That made Dusty laugh, and when he managed to get his slacks and other shoe off, he crashed onto the comforter, howling.

Ben rolled to the side and tickled Dusty, which got the desired response. He sneaked in a hand and grabbed Ben's ribs.

"Whoa! No. No, anything but that?"

"Anything?" His dimples popped as he loomed over Ben.

"Uh, no brussels sprouts."

"Oh really? I love brussels sprouts."

"You would!" He crab-walked away from the tickling fingers.

Dusty hooked a thumb into his blue boxer briefs, and Ben froze. Inch by tantalizing inch, he began dragging them down his hips. The fabric obviously got hung up on a prominent protuberance, but he kept pulling until—*pop!* A more than respectable, long, slim dick slapped against Dusty's flat abdomen.

Ben sighed. "I prefer zucchini."

Dusty tossed the briefs as he dropped the full length of his lean, hard-muscled body on top of Ben. *Oh my God.* The heat of Dusty's skin met the fire of Ben's blood, and everything started to boil.

Ben reached up and slid his fingers into Dusty's silky hair, then pulled his head down so their lips met. *Oh yes.* He tasted like tomato sauce, Ben's dick, and sweetness, which became Ben's new favorite flavor, and he sank in so deep he knew he'd never get out.

Dusty began to rock against Ben, breaking the kiss to slither down so their cocks rubbed like incendiary devices, then crawled back up to kiss some more, since their height difference meant they couldn't kiss and rut their penises at the same time.

While they kissed, Dusty patted a hand around them on the comforter. When he'd managed to grab the lube, he slid back for some dick friction while he slicked up his fingers and reached around his own butt. After some gymnastics getting his fingers in his own hole, he reared back onto his knees and slid a shiny, lubed condom on Ben, then smiled as he scooted over Ben's hips, raised his leg, and balanced like a caveman at a campfire with Ben's cock pointed right at his shiny hole.

Ben couldn't catch his breath.

"Ready?" Dusty's cheeks shone pink and his forehead gleamed with sweat. *So frigging beautiful.*

"All my life."

Dusty's saucy grin softened and his lips parted as he pressed Ben into his body, his eyes closing, light brown lashes fanning against his rose cheeks. "I dreamed of this forever. How can it be so much better than a dream?" He sank to Ben's balls, then rose up, his thigh muscles flexing, dragging perfect pressure and friction over every inch of Ben's cock. It was so intense Ben could hardly believe he was wearing a condom.

Dusty's breath became a moan, then devolved into a grunt as his movements shortened and intensified. He bounced, hair flying like a sunlit sail, his head thrown back, teeth clenched, and his own penis ratcheting up and down so fast Ben couldn't grab it.

Shots of exquisite electricity zapped from Ben's balls up his spine until his brain tingled and fizzed. "Jesus, Dusty."

"Ben, oh my God, Ben."

The perfect experience combined with the effects of long deprivation ended him. "Dusty!" On one deep final thrust, Ben released into a million pieces—

As somewhere on the edge of the universe Dusty yelled, "Yes!"

Ben collapsed and reassembled into a whole new being—one that loved Dusty Kincaid with every piece of his heart.

CHAPTER FOURTEEN

———————

Dusty lay like a happily boiled vegetable on the comforter beside Ben. He hadn't had a seizure, unless you counted his heart now being too big for his chest. *Did I really get to do this? Did I have sex with Ben Shane?* Half his brain screamed that it was a one-time thing. Ben would come to his senses soon. *Shut up. He broke his engagement. He saw me at my worst and didn't run.*

"You're thinking way too hard for a postcoital glow."

Dusty propped his head on his hand. "You really used 'postcoital' in a sentence?"

Ben assumed the same position, gazing at Dusty. "That's me. Mr. Romance."

"Hey, you don't do badly—for an old guy."

Ben snorted, then fiddled with the comforter. "You can't stay, can you?"

"Nah, Mom would worry too much."

Ben nodded and smiled. He was really a nice guy on top of the sex thing. "Let me know when we need to get up and go."

Dusty glanced at Ben's watch. "Soon."

"We need to move you closer so we can sneak you into the bedroom on a moment's notice." He grinned.

Dusty rolled onto his back again and ran a hand over his happy belly—happy because it was in close proximity to his ecstatic balls. "Closer's more expensive, sadly. One-room apartments in Laguna cost more than a whole house in Anaheim. We were lucky to find that place." He sighed before he realized it.

"What?"

Dusty turned his head and looked at Ben. No need to burden Ben with his worries. Besides, the new job would help him afford rent on an apartment, though it still wouldn't be easy. "Oh, nothing, but we may be looking for a new place soon anyway." He smiled, then slowly sat up and stretched. "I hate to say it, but I better get home."

"Do you have time for a shower?"

"Cleanliness is important." Dusty grinned.

"That's what I always say."

A very clean and very sexy half-hour later, Dusty leaned back in Ben's car seat and let the music wash over him like the warm water had.

Ben said, "You mentioned that you used to work construction. Did you like the company you worked for?"

"Oh yes. It was a small group, but they do good work. Construction's not the best for me, because of the power tools and stuff, or I would have stayed. Why?"

"The company that's renovating the house is too busy to give my little job much attention and, uh, I want to get to work on the guest house."

"Oh right. I saw that. What a great place. I can give you the name of the contractor or call him for you."

"Yeah, why don't you call him and ask him to come over and look at the place. Maybe tomorrow after work."

"Sure." *Work. Wow.* A B-2 butterfly dive-bombed his stomach.

Dusty stared at the computer screen on his desk. He giggled. Yes. The words *his* and *desk* were in tandem. If nobody ever gave him another birthday present or Christmas package again, it'd be okay, because he'd gotten the biggest, shiniest, most fantastic gifts the world could offer. Sex with Ben Shane and now this. This job of his wildest dreams. His brain raced in fifty directions, combing a list of epilepsy researchers, looking for sparks of innovation, ideas that would improve quality of life, so many cool things. And he had money to give these researchers! Well, it wasn't his, but he got to recommend where to distribute Mrs. Merced's millions. He laughed. It sounded like a TV soap opera.

He looked up at a tap on the wall of his cubicle. *My cubicle.* A young guy with hair a little darker than his own stood there grinning. Dusty smiled back. "Hi."

"I don't want to bother you."

"No bother. How can I help you?"

"My name's Jesse Randall. I'm Craig Elson's fiancé."

"Oh, I know Craig. He's a really creative guy."

"I think so too." He had cute dimples.

"Want to sit down?"

"Thanks." He slid into the chair that tucked in beside the entrance to Dusty's workspace. "I just want to set up a double date with you and Ben."

"Oh." He heard his own soft gasp.

Jesse cocked his head. "Is that a challenging idea?"

"Sorry." He shook his head. "The idea that I could set up a date for Ben and me is a pretty new concept. I'm not exactly comfortable with it."

"Well, you probably better try it out, because Ben said I should come and ask you." He chuckled.

"He did?"

"Yep. How's this coming weekend?"

"Uh, I—oh."

Jesse gave him that quizzical look again.

"Sorry. I have to look for a new place to live and think about moving with my mom. I'm not sure how long it'll take."

"From and to?"

"From Anaheim. To? No idea."

"Hey, I can help."

"What?"

"Yeah, I know a lot of people in real estate. That's kind of how Craig and I got together. What if maybe I line up some places for, like, Saturday, okay?"

He felt as if a whirlwind had touched down in his cube. Whirlwind Jesse. "Uh, I doubt if a real estate agent will be interested. We hardly have any money. I mean, my new job will help some, but we still can't afford much."

"No worries. I know some cool agents. Give me your phone." He held out a hand.

Dusty chuckled and handed it over.

Jesse tapped away, then said, "This is my number. I sent myself a text so I have yours. I'll tell Ben I'm doing this, and—"

"Uh, no, wait." Jesse looked up. "I don't want to worry Ben. He has enough on his plate."

"Sure. I understand." Jesse stood. "So, do you trust me to help you? I know I'm a stranger."

"Hey, you're not that strange."

They both laughed and bumped fists, and then Jesse waved and walked out, disappearing down the hall.

Add to that amazing list of gifts: help on a place to live and a guy who might turn out to be a friend.

He worked, filled out papers for HR, talked to Trudy about what she wanted him to accomplish, and went back to his computer for another dose of research. Time flew, even if he had to stretch quite a few times since he wasn't used to sitting so much.

The world's most perfect face appeared around the edge of his cubicle. "Sorry I've been missing all day. I had an offsite meeting with a potential donor." Ben smiled as he slid into the chair that Jesse had occupied earlier.

"How did it go?"

"The meeting? Great. He's a friend of Anastasia's."

"Man, meeting her was one lucky day." Dusty smiled.

"Yep, since that was the same day I realized I wanted you."

"You did?"

"Yep. And everything else paled by comparison."

Dusty leaned his head on his hand. "I said you were romantic."

Ben popped his dimples. "Did you talk to Jesse?"

"Oh yes." Dusty straightened.

"Do we have a double date?"

"We're, uh, talking about it."

"Did you get a hold of that contractor?"

"Yes, he's coming in"—he glanced at Ben's watch—"holy cow, a little over an hour. Sorry, I lost track of time."

"No problem. Can you come with me?"

The need to get packing boxes and start looking for available apartments flooded his brain. "I better go home. My mom's expecting me. I told John Harcom—that's his name—your address and generally what you were looking for. He says he's got the manpower and time in his schedule for the project. I think you'll like him."

Ben hopped up. "So come on, let's get you home so I'm not late."

Dusty pushed back from his desk. "That's okay. I can take the bus easily."

"No way. Come on. Let's hoof it. You can tell me how you liked your first day on the way to your mom's house."

He giggled.

"What?"

"Nothing." But he grinned all the way to Ben's car. *So this is what it feels like to have a boyfriend.*

*T*HIS DOES *not feel like I have a boyfriend.* Dusty sipped warm water and lemon and stared around the chaos of packing to the bright Saturday morning outside. A week of effectively no Ben. It wasn't entirely Ben's fault. Dusty had sneaked off two evenings to look at possible apartments, but Ben had been tied up every night with house stuff. After seemingly getting nothing done for months, he now seemed focused on nothing else. *Oh well, focus.* "You sure you don't want to go, Mom?"

His mom unbent from the box she was packing and stretched her back. "No. I need to fill these boxes you got. I trust you. Just find something. Anything." She peered toward the living room window. "So who's the boy you're going with again?"

"His name's Jesse. He's a friend of a friend, but he says he knows some places, so—" He shrugged. "It was nice of him to offer to help."

"Yes. Did you explain our, uh, limited budget?"

"Yes, totally. No worries." He kissed her cheek.

"You're feeling okay?" She gave him the mom look.

"It's funny. Knowing that all those people are researching epilepsy makes me feel better."

"Good. I'm thrilled that you love this new job so much." She looked down and then met his gaze again. "How's it going with Ben?"

The smile spread across his face on its own.

"Okay, I get the idea. It's just that you've been home almost every night this week. No dinners, no kisses in the car. I thought maybe the dew was off the rose." She gave him a little grin.

"I'm not sure I get that whole 'dew' thing, but we're fine. Great. It's just that I've been looking for a place to live, and he's working on his house." He felt the crease in his forehead and consciously smoothed it out. "When things calm down, we'll do some more snuggling."

"Just remember, life's what happens while we're waiting for things to calm down."

"Mom." He smiled softly. "You like Ben." It wasn't a question.

"More important, *you* like Ben. And while I had my doubts, he stepped up and seems like a good man for you. But you should be with him. I can do this."

He heard the car pull up in the driveway and gave his mom another quick peck. "I'll only be a little while. Who knows? Maybe Jesse found something good." He bounded out the door and saw a Nissan Leaf in the driveway with cute Jesse behind the wheel.

Dusty leaned down and waved, then crawled into the passenger seat. "Thank you so much for doing this."

"Hey, my pleasure. I love house hunting."

Two hours later, some of the pleasure was off the project. They'd seen three places—two apartments and a house—but none of them were right.

Jesse pulled his Leaf away from the curb of a house in Garden Grove that turned out to be a nice place but too close to the power lines. The EMI didn't work for Dusty. Jesse said, "Hey. no worries. I've got one more."

"I really appreciate this, Jesse." Dusty rubbed the bridge of his nose. "I know it's hard to find something in our price range. I saw one apartment this past week that'll probably be okay for us. It's just kind of far from work and not close to the bus lines, but it's big enough for me and my mom."

"Yeah, well, don't give up hope yet." Jesse laughed and turned onto Laguna Canyon Road.

They chatted as they drove through the winding, narrow road that crept over the hills that separated Laguna from the rest of Orange County. Suddenly Dusty glanced around. "Wait, uh, where are we going? There's nothing in this direction I can afford now or likely in this life."

"Don't worry. We'll grab some lunch, then keep going."

Dusty settled back and enjoyed the rest of the ride humming to Jesse's collection of Bruno Mars and Maroon 5.

On Broadway, Jesse turned right up the hill—when even Dusty knew almost all the restaurants were to the left. "Uh, Jesse—"

"Ben said to stop by. He might go to lunch with us."

"I thought you weren't going to tell him about the house hunt."

"I didn't. Honest." He glanced at Dusty, then flashed teeth. "He already knew."

"How?" He frowned.

"No idea. I figured you must have decided to tell him."

"No."

"No harm done, right? He'll find out soon enough when he starts picking you up someplace else."

"I guess so." He stared at his hands. He didn't want to

layer one more complication of his life on Ben, but it sure would be fun to see him.

In front of Ben's house, trucks were lined up, and the sounds of hammering and sawing filled the air. *Wow.* He could certainly see what Ben had been spending his time on. No wonder he'd been so busy.

A couple of guys Dusty remembered from his construction days were hauling a big piece of equipment out the front door as he got out of the car. A guy they called Moose nodded as he backed down the stairs. "Hey, Dusty. Thanks for the new job. Great place."

"Uh, hi, Moose."

Jesse walked around the car, and they ambled onto the porch. Dusty peeked in the open front door. The first thing he saw was a nearly done house, or at least the part he could see. Shiny new polished floors, fresh paint, even furniture. "Holy crap, how much did you do in a week?"

Dusty stepped into the entry and looked into the living room. Jesse's fiancé, Craig, stood by the fireplace and— "Mom!" Dusty ran across the room to his mother, who sat on the couch, red-eyed. "How did you get here? What's wrong? Are you okay?"

She snuffled and blew her nose.

From behind Dusty, Ben said, "I think she just said, 'Yes, she's okay.'"

Dusty whirled. "What's going on?"

"Sit." Ben grinned.

Dusty sat next to his mother, who pressed her head against his shoulder and snuffled some more.

Ben said, "I was just showing you mom her new house."

"What? What are you—?" The light dawned. "The guest house?"

"Yes. I've been wondering what I'd do with that nice little

place. My folks live locally, and it's not big enough for two." He shrugged. "Of course, that means there's not really room for you in there, so—" His grin turned into a full-on smile. "I guess you'll be forced to move in with me." His smile faded a little. "If you want to, of course. I don't want to railroad you, but your mom really loves the guest house, so—"

Dusty hurled himself off the couch and into Ben's arms—a near disaster since Ben wasn't ready, but he managed to catch him and remain upright all at the same time. By the time his arms were locked around Ben's neck, the tears he hadn't shed in all the days, years of stress, began to slide down his cheeks.

Ben whispered against Dusty's cheek. "Are those good tears?"

"B-better th-than good."

He felt arms around his back and glanced over his shoulder to see his mom joining the hug. She said, "Don't let us push you, honey. You don't have to do this if you're not ready." She gave him a grin as mischievous as any he'd seen on her face in years. "You can always come and sleep on the couch in the guest house."

He opened his arm and brought her closer. "The first time I saw that house, I wished you could have something as nice."

Ben said, "And, of course, this house does have a guest room I seem to recall you admiring. It could be yours."

Dusty looked up through his lashes and sniffed. "We'll discuss the sleeping arrangements later." He looked over at Jesse and Craig, who sat on the sofa—a beautiful, honey-colored leather sectional just like Dusty would have picked if he'd gone shopping. "How did you do all this?"

Ben said, "Why don't we sit, and I'll explain."

Across from the sectional were two striped easy chairs sitting on an abstract floral rug—an unexpected and perfect combination. Dusty's mom sat in one chair while Ben led Dusty to the couch.

Dusty looked around at the small group. "Were you all in on this?"

His mom shook her head. "Not exactly. Ben called me and told me he knew we were losing our house and he'd like to help." She gave Ben a cheeky half smile. "I told him no way. We'd gotten along fine on our own for twenty-three years, and we'd keep on doing it."

Ben sorted. "She's tough."

Dusty laughed. "Got that right."

His mom said, "But he told me if I'd stop being a tiger mom for one minute, I'd see that it was best for us to take some help. He said he really loved you and wanted to give you a better life."

She might have kept on talking, but Dusty stared at Ben.

Ben looked at him. "What?"

"Love?" The tears popped out again.

"No, I want you to move in so you can supervise construction."

Dusty's mouth fell open.

"Of course I love you. Do you think I would've spent a week cracking the whip on these guys to get my place done and ready for you if I didn't care? I loved you that day Craig caught me staring at your ass—excuse me, Laurie. I just didn't know it yet."

Dusty giggled. "Well, I've been told I have a lovable ass. Excuse me, Mother." He looked back and forth between Ben and his mom. "So you know my mom's first name?"

"Oh yes, we've had many communications since she told me to suck eggs."

"Which time?" Dusty laughed.

Jesse said, "Hang on. You can't change topics while we're still in suspense."

Craig nodded. "Right."

"Dusty, do you love Ben back, ass and all?" Jesse chuckled.

Dusty slowly inhaled and looked up into Ben's perfect face. "I don't even know how to tell you how much. I'd call you a dream come true, but I never could have dreamed of anyone so perfect." He pressed his nose against Ben's neck and inhaled sweetness. "I can't believe you'd want to take on— me. I realize you don't fully know what that means, but I'll work every day to be the kind of partner you deserve."

Ben tipped up Dusty's chin. "You don't have to work, Dusty. You *are* the one for me, just by being you. In fact, I want you to work less and have more joy."

Dusty's mom wiped some more tears. "That's the best medicine I can think of."

Dusty smiled at her, still snuggled against Ben's chest. "I seem to recall you were at home when I left today."

"Ben called right after Jesse picked you up. He said he was on his way to get me. I didn't know about the guest house until I got here." She swiped at her cheeks. "I still can't believe it. Have you seen it?"

"Not lately." Dusty looked around. "I don't even recognize this house."

Ben said, "We'll take a tour and then go to lunch to celebrate." He looked up. "Laurie, why don't you show Jesse and Craig your place, and Dusty and I will be right out."

She beamed. "I'd love to."

When they were all happily flocking out the back door, Ben turned to Dusty. "I just want to make sure we're not overwhelming you with expectations. I want you to be certain this is what you want."

Dusty gazed into Ben's deep green eyes. "I wasn't kidding. I could never have said this is what I want because I couldn't get myself to dream this big. But yes, Ben. I can't imagine a more perfect life." He inhaled slowly.

"Then let me show you your room." He took Dusty's hand and led him down the hall, then opened the door on the newly renovated master suite.

"Whoa." Soft midday light filtered through sheer curtains onto the huge bed covered in crisp, white sheets and a big, fluffy comforter folded at the foot. The two chairs by the window each had their own comfy throw tucked over the arm. Dusty sniffled.

Ben laughed and pulled Dusty across the room, where he opened the closet door with a flourish. Yes, it was a whole room and was just as luxurious as it had been, but now one whole side had been cleared of clothes.

"Uh, do you think there's room for my three pairs of jeans and five T-shirts?"

"We're going to correct that." Ben picked him up and spun him.

"Whoa. Am I supposed to be the second clotheshorse?" When his feet hit the ground, he looked at Ben with all the seriousness he could muster under these fairy-tale circumstances. "Ben, are you sure? Being with a person with epilepsy isn't a picnic. It's hard to relax and feel calm and safe."

"I know. Your mom's told me a lot."

He shook his head. "You guys have sure been busy. But you do realize, right, that anyone who heard what you gave up in exchange for what you're getting would say you're mad." He smiled softly.

Ben tipped Dusty's chin up. "No, they wouldn't. Not when they heard that I love you so madly." And he closed the deal with his lips.

Want more from Tara Lain?
Download Tara Lain's Beautiful Boys of Romance, Sample
Book FREE on Prolific Works

Sign up for Tara's newsletter to keep in the loop about new
releases, sales, and more.
bit.ly/TaraLainNews

KEEP READING

Keep Reading for an Excerpt from LOVE YOU SO SPECIAL, a Love You So Novel by Tara Lain

Artie Haynes put the last twist on the nut connecting the supply tube to the tailpiece under the sink in the big men's room. Like always, he suppressed a chuckle at the double meaning in the names of the plumbing parts. He never shared the joke. The guys might be big on tail, but they sure as hell weren't into nuts.

Martinez peered in the door. Soft music filtered through along with his tough-guy face. "Yo, Haynes. Ya done? Wanna go get a beer?"

Did he? He liked beer and he liked the guys well enough, but he only had one more day on this job. That meant one more day when he could sneak into the back of the giant auditorium and listen to those people play music—music like he'd barely ever heard before. "Nah. Thanks, man. Gotta do some family shit."

Martinez snorted. "Tell me about it. You ain't seen family crap till you've been Mexican, man. See ya tomorrow." The door closed behind him.

Artie leaned under the sink and turned the water back on,

stripped off his gloves, and stuck them in his tool bag. The damned thing weighed a ton, but he didn't like leaving his tools behind at the job like some guys did. Hefting the bag on his shoulder, he stepped out into the wide hall beside the men's room he and the crew had been renovating. The client had only given them three days to get the work done in there since they needed the bathroom for some big concert. He would have liked to stay twice as long.

The music filled the hall, though it stopped sometimes and then restarted. The previous day Artie had watched the guy up front of that big band click his stick and everybody'd stop. The leader would say some stuff Artie couldn't hear from the back, and then the players would go back and do it again. Maybe that dude heard something wrong, but man, to Artie's ears it sounded perfect.

The music began again, and real quietly Artie slipped into the back of the big auditorium, set his tool bag on the floor, and then hunkered down in a seat near the exit doors. Two or three other people were sitting in the hall listening, but they were up front.

Artie leaned his head against the back of the seat and let the music wash over him like the world's best shower. *Wonder what that music's called?* It was real complicated, with lots of instruments playing at once, but they went together so perfect. It was, like, unexpected. The horn things would play something and then the fiddles would pick it up. *Wow. Imagine being able to make music like that.*

In his pocket, his phone vibrated once. *Text.* He didn't even look. It could wait. This was too great.

"Are you enjoying the music?"

Artie was on his feet so fast he got light-headed. A small, white-haired woman in beautiful clothes stood beside him in the aisle. She must be a damned ninja, because he hadn't heard her coming. "Uh, yes ma'am, I am. I hope I'm not bothering anyone."

She waved a hand sporting a diamond the size of a bagel. "Not at all. We're always happy to know our audiences are enjoying the symphony."

"It's really great." He didn't mention that he was as likely to be a member of the audience at Sanderson Hall as he was to turn into Superman. He'd seen the prices on those tickets.

"I noticed you were here yesterday as well." She was smiling, so she didn't look pissed about it.

He grinned back. People always said his dimples were his best feature. "I'm part of the crew working on the renovations. I'm the plumber, although I do carpentry too. I can hear the music from across the hall, and it's hard to resist." He held up a hand. "I'm all done for the day, so I'm on my own time."

She laughed. "You don't have to punch a time clock for me. Music is at least as important as work."

He nodded. "Yeah. It's like food or something. You hear it and you feel—better. Sorry, I haven't got the right words."

"You're doing fine." She stuck out her hand. "I'm Helen Sanderson, by the way."

He stared like maybe some angel had descended from heaven. *Damn, I hope my hands are clean.* He shook her hand. It felt tiny and soft. "Artie Haynes." *Wait.* "Did you say Sanderson?"

"Yes. My family built this hall." She laughed, and it sounded pretty musical. "They paid to have it built, of course. No hammers involved. That's your job. So please feel free to drop by anytime."

"Uh, ma'am. Can you tell me what that music is?"

She looked a little surprised but nodded. "Yes, it's

Beethoven's Fifth Symphony. One of the most popular of Beethoven's works. Do you like it?"

"Yeah. I mean, yes. I really like it a lot."

"I hope you'll come and see it performed when they've finished rehearsing. That won't be until later in the year. The season doesn't really start until fall, except for special events."

"Oh, uh, thanks." At least he had one more day to listen to them practice.

"It's been a pleasure, Artie. I'm always glad to meet a fellow music lover." She patted his arm. "Will you be here tomorrow?"

"Yes, ma'am."

"Be sure and come in to listen, because we have an extraordinary soloist I think you'll enjoy."

Soloist? "Uh, like a singer?"

She smiled. "No, he's a pianist. Truly exceptional. The only way we got him is because he's local, so they made a small exception for us." She lowered her voice. "Honorarium-wise." She gave a little laugh.

He smiled back, though he had no clue what that meant.

"I hope I see you again." She walked out the auditorium doors.

What a cool lady. He glanced toward the stage. It looked like the musicians were closing up their stuff, so Artie grabbed his tool bag and left before anybody else noticed him. It took a couple of minutes to walk through the halls to the back entrance they kept open during the day and out into the sun of a southern California afternoon.

So, something cool was going to happen tomorrow. A little shiver ran up his back. If today's music was just your regular and tomorrow's was special, shit, he couldn't wait.

Oh right, the text. He stepped against the wall into the shade and brought it up.

Hey Artie. Got a job for you starting Monday if you're free. Needs carpentry and plumbing. A little electrical. Private home. Probably a couple weeks work at least. Let me know quick. JT.

JT Morrow was one of the small contractors Artie worked for. *Good guy.* Honest and paid decent. Perfect timing too since this job finished the next day. That meant he could pick up a bartender gig on the weekend and maybe take a day off. *Man, that'd be different.*

Artie typed, *I'm in. Text me the details.*

Shoving the phone into his pocket, he walked to his battered truck, then drove up the on-ramp to the ridiculously crowded 405 freeway. He always wanted to say *Come on, guys. It's three in the afternoon. Give us working stiffs a break.* But no such luck. After a lot of stop and start, he veered onto the even worse 55 freeway, then, when the damned cars went nowhere, pulled off the freeway onto a side street to try to outmaneuver the crush on his way to his apartment over a garage in Costa Mesa. Finally he pulled into the driveway. Don Rogers, the old man who lived in the house in front of the apartment, was out puttering in his yard.

Artie waved. "Hey, Don, need any help?"

At eighty-two Don had slowed down a little, but he kept himself fit with walks and lots of messing in his yard. He owned the house outright, so renting to Artie gave him a little income to supplement his Social Security and pension from his job as a teacher. Artie took care of his own maintenance and a lot of Don's too, but he still insisted on paying full rent. Hell, Don needed it more than him.

"Thanks, Artie. I'm good for today. I'll be making enough for two at dinner if you want to join."

"Oh, thanks. I'm going to go visit the parental unit."

Artie laughed. They'd heard that expression in a movie

they'd watched together, and Don always got a kick out of it so Artie always used it.

Don said, "I can save you some."

"Likely they'll feed me. But thanks."

Don nodded. "Come get it later if you're hungry." He knew how bad Artie's mom's cooking was, since Artie complained about it enough.

Artie waved and ran up the stairs to his place. Inside, he tossed his jacket on the lounger with the cracked phony leather, then crouched in front of his fucking fish tank. That's what he called it because he'd been sucked in by a bunch of fucking fish. He smiled and ran a hand across the glass. A couple of the little fuckers came up and nibbled against the other side. *Too cute.*

He'd won a bowl with a goldfish in it at a fair, so he went to a store to buy some food. *Bad idea.* He saw these fish, like a painting in a tank—neon blue, orange and black stripes, fat little black guys. He told the person at the store he wanted a couple of those. The person told him those were tropical fish and he'd need air and filters and shit. But those little fuckers sucked him in, and he walked out of there with a two-hundred-dollar bill, six fish, and a weekend's worth of work setting it all up. Yeah, and he never told anybody, but he loved them. Actually looked forward to coming home just to see them. *Pathetic.*

He rose and stepped to the table where he kept the small aquarium. He stuck his finger in, and the goldfish sucked on it and his girlfriend rushed over to do her own kissing. He gave them a little food. *GG. Gateway Goldfish. Shee-it.*

He hurried into the bathroom for a shower and quick change. If he got to his parents early enough, maybe he could get away and have time for a beer before he turned in. He wanted to get to the job early tomorrow.

The water running over his head felt good. He didn't like to run up Don's water bill, but just a couple of minutes. He sighed. It'd be nice to jerk off, but he'd wait until tonight and relax himself to sleep.

A couple of minutes later, he was dry, in clean jeans and a long-sleeved T-shirt that was dark red. Yeah, it was a weird color for a guy, but it felt a little bit—he shrugged as he pulled it on—special. And it looked good with his light brown hair and brown eyes.

He made a rude razzberry noise. *Give it up. You're wading into deep water, man. You're gonna start watching* Project Runway *soon.*

When he ran back down his stairs, Don was inside. Artie could see him through the kitchen window. He waved and hauled ass into his truck. *Get this done.*

His parents' house was only about ten minutes from his apartment, but where his place was in east-side Costa Mesa, a pleasant area that got ocean breezes and had a nice mix of old and new houses, his folks' home was on the west side, definitely rougher and run-down. When he pulled up in front, it was like going back in time. They'd lived there since before he, his brother, and sister were born, and it never changed except to get uglier. It was like his folks figured houses were supposed to wear out like people did, and hopefully the building made it as long as the bodies.

He climbed out of his truck and eyed the roof. Roofing was no specialty of his, but if he couldn't figure out a way to do it, they'd be lucky not to be watching TV in the rain.

The front door opened. "Yo, bro!" His brother, AB—a nickname he got since somehow the folks had gone Biblical when he showed up and named him Abraham—ran out the door, leaped through the air, and tackled Artie, sending them both careening backward toward the truck. Since AB was smaller, Artie managed to keep his feet, but it was a near thing. Not that he shouldn't have been ready. AB greeted him someway similar every time he came to visit.

Artie grinned. "Hey, man." AB managed to be his friend, despite their being not very much alike. Of course, AB didn't quite know that. He gave AB a short punch on the arm. "How's it?"

AB shrugged. "Same ol'."

Yeah, that described their family all right.

AB snorted. "What's with the shirt?"

"Oh, uh, haven't done laundry."

"Yeah. Looks like it." He slapped Artie's shoulder.

Artie threw an arm around AB's neck, and they walked through the open front door directly into the living room. Until he'd started working on other people's houses, Artie barely realized there was such a thing as an entry.

His dad sat in a recliner, feet up, paunch hanging over his belt, which Artie could clearly see in his white T-shirt. He had a beer on the side table and was gazing at the TV, where some football game played. Across the small room, in "her chair," his mother wore her favorite tights and a T-shirt. A romance novel was held open in her left hand and her right held a Diet Coke, a drink she was more addicted to than his dad was to beer, and that was saying something. The carpet in front of both chairs, that had once been some shade of blue now looked dull gray-brown, not as much from dirt as wear. She glanced up. "Hi, honey."

"Hi, Mom." He leaned over and kissed the cheek she held his way.

"You staying for dinner?"

"Uh, I better not. I've got some work stuff to finish up."

She pulled her glasses off. "You work too hard."

"Nah. You know how it is. Best to take the jobs when you can get them." His mom worked as a cook in a high school cafeteria while his dad had been night shift at a supermarket for as long as Artie could remember. He sat on the couch they'd covered with an old blanket. Junior, their ancient black lab, opened one eye at him, then sighed and returned to sleep. Artie patted him. "I just wanted to see how you are."

"Same old, same old. What's with the shirt?"

AB piped in, "He didn't do laundry."

"Looks like it."

Artie didn't sigh. "How's work, Dad?"

His father dragged his eyes from the big TV, the one thing in the house they kept up to date. "Good. I mean, nothing special, but then, what's new about that?" He laughed, but it didn't sound funny. "How about you?"

Artie leaned back on the couch even though it made the blanket fall down behind his back. "Good. I have this job at the Sanderson Center." Neither parental unit flickered an eyelash at that. "You know, that big place over by the Plaza shopping center where they do music and plays and shit?"

"Oh yeah, kind of."

AB nodded. "Right. I've seen that place. Kind of cool."

Artie smiled. "Yeah, well, I've been working in there, and they have all these musicians who play in an orchestra. Real fancy stuff like violins and giant violins and horns that are huge. Anyway, they play this amazing music, and you can hear it all over the whole building and—" His father's eyes wandered back to the TV, AB's leg bounced, and his mom stared at her book. Artie let out his breath real slow. "Who's playing, Dad?"

"Rams, man. You oughta know that. You really must've been working too hard." He laughed.

Artie started scratching Junior's ear, stared at the television, and spent the next half hour commenting on every play every Ram made. He was way up to date on the team, not because he really loved football that much, but because every other person in his life did. Finally he felt like he'd done enough father/son bonding shit. He rose. "I better get going. Yell if you need anything."

His dad glanced up, then back at the screen. "Great to see you. I'll let you know how the game turns out."

"Thanks." He noogied AB's head. "Take care, squirt." AB was only two years younger, but he hadn't quite gotten it together enough to move out, unlike Artie who'd rented a room at sixteen and spent the last nine years on his own. Artie leaned over and gave his mom another quick kiss.

She glanced up. "Oh, you gotta go, sweetie?"

"Yeah. I'll see you soon."

"Okay, dear." She patted his cheek but was looking back at the page before he even stood up. At least she liked to read.

AB walked to the truck with him. Artie said, "You okay? You need anything?"

"Yeah. Pretty much. I've got a few construction jobs coming up, 'cause shit, man, who can live on what I make at Taco Heaven?"

Artie dug in his pocket, grabbed some bills he had ready, and handed them to AB. "Here. This'll tide you over until you get those jobs."

"Oh, you don't have to, man. I know you haven't got much left over." But he already had the money moving toward his pocket. "Thanks, bro. You're great."

"No problem. See you soon." He gave AB a one-armed hug, then walked around the truck and slid in. Fact was, the money was to ease his guilty conscience. He'd gotten AB a job once with one of his contractors, and he'd done such a crappy job, the contractor hardly let Artie forget it. Now, Artie gave AB money—but no jobs.

With a long, easy breath, he pulled away from the curb and pointed the truck straight for his buddies' favorite bar. After a beer maybe he'd do a little work, just so he wouldn't have lied to his dad. Hell, he hated to add one more lie.

MEET TARA LAIN

Tara Lain believes in happy ever afters - and magic. Same thing. In fact, she says, she doesn't believe, she knows. Tara shares this passion in her stories that star her unique, charismatic heroes and adventurous heroines. Quarterbacks and cops, werewolves and witches, blue collar or billionaires, Tara's characters, readers say, love deeply, resolve seemingly insurmountable differences, and ultimately live their lives authentically. After many years living in southern California, Tara, her soulmate honey and her soulmate dog decided they wanted less cars and more trees, prompting a move to Ashland, Oregon where Tara's creating new stories and loving living in a small town with big culture. Likely a Gryffindor or maybe a Ravenclaw but possessed of Parseltongue, Tara loves animals of all kinds, diversity, open minds, coconut crunch ice cream from Zoeys, and her readers. She also loves to hear from you.

Come visit my website for a FREE download of my Sample Book. https://taralain.com/

If you like to stay up to date on books in general and mine in particular, come join my Reader Group, HEA, Magic, and Beautiful Boys

https://www.facebook.com/
groups/TaraLainsHEAMagicAndBeautifulBoys/

Subscribe to my Newsletter and get a drawing for fun prizes in every issue -- https://bit.ly/TaraLainNews

Follow me on Amazon for all the new releases, and on Bookbub for specials and to see the books that I love.

Of course, you'll find me on Facebook, Twitter, Pinterest, and Instagram

facebook.com/taralain

twitter.com/taralain

instagram.com/taralainauthor

bookbub.com/authors/tara-lain

amazon.com/author/tara-lain

goodreads.com/goodreadscomtara_lain

BOOKS BY TARA LAIN

From Tara Lain Books – Available in KU

<u>NERDS VS JOCKS</u> (with Eli Easton)

Schooling the Jock

Coaching the Nerd

Head to Head

<u>MOVIE MAGIC ROMANCES</u>

Return of the Chauffeur's Son

Love and Linguistics

<u>DANGEROUS DANCERS</u>

Golden Dancer

Dangerous Dancer

<u>COWBOYS DON'T</u>

Cowboys Don't Come Out

Cowboys Don't Ride Unicorns

Cowboys Don't Samba

<u>LOVE IN LAGUNA</u>

Knight of Ocean Avenue

Knave of Broken Hearts

Prince of the Playhouse

Lord of a Thousand Steps

Fool of Main Beach

LOVE YOU SO

Love You So Hard

Love You So Madly

Love You So Special

Love You So Sweetly

THE MIDDLEMARK MYSTERIES

The Case of the Sexy Shakespearean

The Case of the Voracious Vintner

PENNYMAKER TALES SERIES

Sinders and Ash

Driven Snow

Beauty, Inc

Never

THE ALOYSIUS TALES SERIES

Spell Cat

Brush with Catastrophe

Cataclysmic Shift

EVER AFTER, NEW YORK STORIES

Better Red

Holding Hans

FUZZY LOVE

Passions of a Papillon

Prancing of a Papillon

BALLS TO THE WALL

Volley Balls

Fire Balls

Beach Balls

FAST Balls

High Balls

Snow Balls

Bleu Balls

Hair Balls

TALES OF THE HARKER PACK

The Pack or the Panther

Wolf in Gucci Loafers

Winter's Wolf

LONG PASS CHRONICLES

Outing the Quarterback

Canning the Center

Tackling the Tight End

GENETIC ATTRACTION SERIES

The Scientist and the Supermodel

Genetic Attraction

The Pretty Boy and the Tomboy

Genetic Celebrity

<u>HOLIDAY NOVELLAS</u>

Mistletowed

Be Bad, For Goodness Sake

<u>STANDALONE TITLES</u>

Home Improvement - A Love Story

Fairy Shop

Taylor Maid

Rome and Jules

Hearts and Flour

<u>SUPERORDINARY SOCIETY</u>

Hidden Powers

Rising Magic

Audiobooks by Tara Lain available at Audible, Amazon, and
Audiobooks.com